Freedom

F-WORD
BOOK FIVE

E. DAVIES

Freedom / E. Davies. – 1st ed.
ISBN: 978-1-912245-23-9

Freedom

CHAPTER

One

JADEN

"I really hate you," Jaden flatly informed Spence.

As always, his big brother crossed his eyes and stuck out his tongue. "Teddy bear don't care."

His brother might look like one, but as far as Jaden was concerned, the nickname was misleading at best. What kind of big brother would drag him out of the house to a gay club for a charity raffle?

Sure, the gesture *seemed* supportive, but Spence knew better. Or he should, by now. Jaden had been fighting back waves of anxiety since Spence brought up the prospect.

Jaden's therapist would be happy he had taken a chance and gotten out of the house, but at what price? His mental state for a few days? A week? And then there was the even bigger problem.

He hissed under his breath, "What if I *win*?" That would mean going out somewhere.

Best case scenario, a nice cozy restaurant. He felt safe enough in his car to cope with the drive. As long as he kept his eyes on his feet when he walked between his car and a building, he could cope. Maybe. He'd nearly passed out between the taxi and the bar tonight.

Spence looked far more at home here, which just wasn't fair since he was straight as an arrow. Jaden might have appreciated his willingness to come to Buckle with him if he'd felt as relaxed as his big brother. As it was, his nerves were frayed just trying to keep himself from running out the door.

Spence had always been a shield for him—on the rare occasions Jaden did leave the house for longer than a grocery trip, Spence was usually at his side. If not for his big brother moving to Denver after the second nervous breakdown, Jaden never would have made it this long.

Didn't mean he should be meddling with anything that didn't concern him, though—like Jaden's love life. Or his mental health recovery. God, brothers could be so irritating.

Spence ignored his question with a good-natured roll of his eyes. Winning hadn't occurred to him, apparently. "I just think you could do with a positive reason to get out of the house. Didn't your therapist say that? The more you shut down, the more anxious you get? Like a spiral to the bottom of social interaction."

Damn it, he was right. Jaden had been slowly pushing himself this year, trying to prove to himself that he was safe so he could use that as evidence to create a *positive* spiral. And he'd made the mistake of sharing some of his insights with Spence, who was pretty much his only visitor at home.

Jaden, rooted on his chair in the corner of the bar, glared at Spence. "For that, you owe me the next drink. The usual."

Spence grinned. "Rum and Coke? Dude, that was your college drink. Aren't you ever going to graduate?"

"I'm in a big, spacious bar with lots of… space. And people." Jaden flatly glared. "Comfort drinks are fine."

At least Spence knew when he'd pushed it a little too far. "Gotcha." He saluted and headed to the bar. No sooner had he reached it than yet another guy approached Jaden's brother with a hopeful smile.

Watching Spence politely reject them as onlookers tried to figure his type out, not even suspecting him of being a straight guy at ease in his sexuality, was normally hilarious. Or it had been, four years ago, when he was just-turned-twenty-one and Spence had brought him here.

Now, Jaden was too busy fighting back the dizzying wave of anxiety at the space, the noise, the lights and music. Luckily, the music had been kept low compared to the bars he'd once partied in—before his nervous breakdown. They could talk without yelling. If not for that, he might have left already.

His agoraphobia wasn't a fear of strangers, exactly. But it had developed rapidly in just the last few years.

Jaden wasn't sure if it was the rum and Cokes or the anxiety making his stomach rumble. Maybe he just needed French fries.

Nearby, a guy was raising his voice. "If you're straight, what are you even doing here?"

That got Jaden's attention—and his protectiveness. But the other guy wasn't addressing Spence. The man he talked to looked unfazed as he grinned back. There was a handsome guy next to him—but damn, he was probably this man's boyfriend. "Helping out a friend."

"Oh, sure." Someone tittered. "You better not be entering any raffles yourself, straight boy. No breaking one of our hearts."

The other guy isn't his boyfriend? Jaden's hope rose as he stood up, not quite sure what had come over him. But he couldn't stand the thought of someone talking to Spence like that when he'd been nice enough to coax Jaden out of his shell tonight. So he wouldn't let anyone talk to this guy that way, either.

"H-Hey. He's okay. Leave him be."

The guys who were addressing him rolled their eyes. "Sure, stand up for him. But don't call us when he breaks your heart," one of them muttered. The other man caught Jaden's eye for a moment and smiled at him. Then he said something to his straight friend and headed to the bar.

Jaden blushed at the brief eye contact, suddenly hot under the collar for more than one reason. He rolled his eyes and sat down again, still a little shaky. He could hardly believe he'd actually had the nerve to speak up there.

But if someone had spoken up when *he'd* most needed it…

"Thanks for that. Can I take this?" The guy he'd helped nodded at the empty chair. "I saw your, um… the other guy walking away, and you looked a little upset. Lover's spat?"

Something about this man seemed trustworthy. He had a short beard obscuring a squared jawline, and a warm glow in his eyes. He looked sympathetic, even concerned, not oily and flirtatious. He wasn't hitting on him.

Jaden relaxed and nodded. "Brothers. He's my big bro. He's straight, too. He just dragged me to this raffle." There were five dates altogether being raffled off, and he tried to reassure himself that he wouldn't actually win any of them.

"Oh!" The stranger cast a bemused glance between the two of them, and then smiled. "So he's just keeping you company?"

"Yes, because he's a *great* brother," Jaden muttered, rolling his eyes. If he could get his stomach to stop jumping through itself like a game of cat's cradle, he might even think the guy was cute. But he so wasn't Jaden's type. Then again, it wasn't like Jaden had *had* a type for the past few years.

"To get you a date?"

"No, to audition as a go-go boy." Oops. That came out a bit more sarcastic than he'd meant. Jaden gave him an apologetic smile. "Uh, yeah. Sorry."

The stranger didn't take it hard, though. "Trip," he introduced himself. "I'm here with a coworker. Same deal. He wanted to say hi, but he was worried that your brother over there was your boyfriend. I was coming over to snoop on you." He gave an unrepentant grin.

Jaden blinked with surprise and then shook his head. "Well, I'm not dating anyone. I'll go on *one* date—if I win the date—and that's it. Back to my apartment and peace and quiet."

Trip coughed into his fist. "Right," he said, his eyes glimmering with amusement. "I see your brother scored drinks. Thanks for the rescue there. Good luck tonight."

As he walked off, Jaden tried to watch him to see if the handsome guy had come back. Not that he was interested. Just for the sake of curiosity.

"Hey! Just about to start," Spence declared loudly in his ear, making him lose track of the big guy. Damn it.

Spence set down four drinks. When Jaden stared, he grinned. "Three guys tried to buy me a drink, and I wasn't going to say no. One of them kissed me and his stubble exfoliated my nose. Not sure I should use the bathroom in the next hour, or I might have company. So, any idea what you want me to bid on?"

Jaden snorted with laughter. Spence's relentless cheerfulness kept him briefly distracted. "I told you—"

"Yeah, yeah. Don't waste your money, you said. Except it all goes to charity, so it's not a waste. Come on. Don't make me choose a raffle box for you."

Jaden groaned and stood up. "I'm too anxious to do this." Any of the dates being raffled off sounded like too much for him. The Heart2Heart charity could keep his money and he'd just leave.

"Hey, man." Spence pressed on his shoulder gently. "If you really hate it, we can go. But I think you can do this. You might not even win. If you do, it's just one date. And if you hate it, you never have to do it again," he added.

Jaden sighed. "Okay," he finally murmured. "Fine. Pick something for me."

Spence had a certain impish grin on his face. "Will do! Drink up!"

Boy, Jaden hoped he didn't regret it.

***

His regrets came home to roost only two hours later.

"And moving on to our final prize! Oh, this box is *full*, people. That's what I said last weekend," the MC cracked jokes as people groaned good-naturedly.

An elbow in his side made Jaden wince and almost spill his drink. "Hey!"

"This is your chance," Spence whispered with a big thumbs-up and grin.

Jaden considered telling him where to stick that thumb. He decided against it and just rolled his eyes. "Shhh."

"What's your number?"

Jaden pulled out the ticket Spence had handed him after heading over to drop the other half in the box.

036. One ticket in a great big box. What were the chances?

The crowd was thick, but the atmosphere was upbeat and happy. And everyone here was smiling at Jaden as they passed, like he was an old friend. It helped keep Jaden's nerves in check.

The first four dates had already been raffled, and he was free and clear. Tickets for some VIP box at a sports arena, theater tickets, a five-star seafood restaurant, cocktails and a few hours in a giant ball pit. Safe from all of those things. All that remained was the fifth and final grand prize.

Of course Spence had chosen to put Jaden's ticket into that box, the asshole. The grand prize was an overnight trip to the Grand Canyon. Helicopter trip, then biking to a picnic and a romantic cabin for two overnight.

Jaden leveled another glare at his brother while the MC cranked up the suspense, but Spence smirked and pretended not to see him.

"210. Do we have a 210 around here?"

A whoop and holler greeted him, and Jaden let out a breath of relief. His chances were even lower. One down, one to go.

"And... I know you're all on the edge of your seat here... how about 36? Zero-three-six, everyone."

"Shit," Spence breathed out.

Jaden froze. Time itself seemed to halt for a moment as he stared at his ticket like it was lying to him.

No. He couldn't do this.

Jaden was out of his seat—and the bar—before he even

knew it. He made it to the cool, fresh air of the sidewalk before he sat on the curb, head in his hands.

Spence was still in there, no doubt getting all the information on his behalf.

This *was* what Jaden had wanted—but not *yet*. Not like this, with a stranger and an overnight trip and the freaking Grand Canyon!

"Oh, my God," Jaden mumbled, pressing the heels of his hands into his eyes until sparks danced across his vision. "What has he done?"

CHAPTER
Two

HENRY

"It'll be good for you." Trip sounded annoyingly cheerful, as everyone who ever said that phrase did. But he wasn't finished. "Getting laid will help with all that broodiness you have going on. Though *that* might actually help with getting laid. I hear the guys love a good Blue Steel."

"Oh, shut up." Henry dumped everything out of his backpack, then balled up his old boxers and threw them at his coworker.

Trip dodged and laughed. "Gross. I smelled you enough for one week. Time for a new loverboy to take on that duty."

"I don't know why I'm agreeing to this," Henry muttered. Being grumpy was a lot easier than admitting to the nervousness that made his heart pound and hands tremble.

They'd only just gotten back from three days in the backcountry of Colorado, right in time for Henry's flight. He and his mysterious date were flying to Phoenix first, then being driven in a limo to the canyon. Fancy as hell.

Trip had dropped Henry off at home, but unfortunately

he'd stuck around to harass him under the guise of helping him pack.

"Because you need a hot man in your life."

"Do I?" Henry scratched the back of his neck as he opened his closet and shoved aside the hangers of water-proof layers and thermal wear.

What did he wear to hike and bike around the Grand Canyon with a total stranger he wanted to impress?

Agreeing to let Trip choose a date for him in the raffle had been a bold move. Hell, agreeing to go to this event at all had been.

"I don't know." Trip's tone was more serious this time. "Do you?"

Henry paused and looked over his shoulder for a moment. Trip was a smart guy, and he had a big heart. It meant a lot that he'd never batted an eye at Henry being gay. But even so, he'd never told Trip that he was trans.

For the last few years, Henry had been living stealth—without telling anyone his history. Everyone knew him as a guy now. With no inconvenient ties with his past life to haunt him, he was just treated like any other guy.

For the most part, he loved it. No barrage of well-meaning but wrongheaded questions about *when he knew* or *why he had to do it*. Nobody treating him differently or tiptoeing around him.

Henry deserved the same amount of privacy as anyone else. He wouldn't dream of asking Trip if he was circumcised or their boss, Damien, what his embarrassing childhood nickname had been. Why should anyone else ask him that kind of stuff?

But there was the inconvenient fact that his transness had become some big secret without his really meaning it to. He didn't exactly *want* it to be a secret. He just didn't want people associating him with the person the world had once mistaken him for. That lie was dead and gone. This was his truth.

But try explaining that to a stranger on Grindr who just wanted to know if he was a top or a bottom, and how big his dick was. Anything outside that box? Too complicated for them. It was even scarier to contemplate losing Trip as a friend over it.

Maybe this date was all too much of a risk. But he was committed now. Too late to turn around.

"Shit, I dunno," was Henry's conclusion.

That made Trip laugh as he crossed his ankles and leaned back. "I think you're running from something."

"Ouch. Thanks, but I'll skip the psychotherapy." Henry mock-grimaced. He'd had quite enough of that for one lifetime.

Trip chuckled gently. "Yeah. But aren't we all, really? Everyone's running from something. Even our guests. What better place to hide than nature?"

"Now you sound like a stoner in the woods. This outing really got to you. Go home and sleep it off," Henry teased Trip with a grin.

Trip raised his hands in defeat and stood up, wandering out of the room. "Message received. At least try to have fun, huh?"

He looked so dejected that Henry felt bad. He turned and half-hugged Trip before he could go. "Thanks, man. I will," he promised. He *was* grateful for the push Trip had given him to get out there and date. "I just… doubt I'll strike it lucky."

"Why don't you think you will?"

Henry made a face. For all he knew, he'd end up paired

with some super-macho insecure guy he'd never in a million years come out to while alone in a cabin. Or a thirty-something professional in a suit with his life together and a string of gorgeous exes.

As a man who had been off the market for months, Henry was more than a little intimidated.

"I don't even know if I'm his type," he said instead. That was a lot simpler than explaining everything.

"Nobody ever knows that. But you gotta take the chance to find out," Trip told him, the gloom fading into another smile. "And, objectively, you're super hot. Even I can recognize that. You can't argue, because I'm an unbiased judge."

Henry cracked up and smacked Trip's shoulder. "You're just trying to get me to cover your vacation this year."

"Maaaybe." Trip winked and shouldered his jacket, grabbing his car keys. "Anyway, have all the fun and tell me about it later."

Henry eyed Trip and shook his head. The rascal was just trying to make him blush. "Go on, get," he shooed Trip, but he was grinning. "See you next week."

Packing went a lot quicker without Trip harassing him, but his friend had gotten the wheels turning.

Was Henry running from something? If so, what? Vulnerability, the weight of his own expectations, or the very real possibilities of rejection and harm… those were all possibilities.

Dating wasn't easy for anyone, but being a trans gay man seemed to add another layer of hoops to jump through. Henry got plenty of interest, which was good for his ego, but turning that into a date… that was where it all fell apart.

Henry had halfheartedly tried for the last year, which mostly consisted of late nights on Grindr when he was in the city between work trips, followed by deleting the app and sharing a bottle of wine with his angst.

Some guys seemingly hadn't cared, but Henry had psyched himself out before they ever met. Others just went silent. A few had jumped straight into genital questions that made Henry want to curl up and never date again.

Adding "trans" to his profile ahead of time to screen out those jerks was no better. Even if he added "top" too, he still got messages from guys who wanted him to bottom because he was trans, or who even thought he was a trans woman.

It was an anxiety-inducing mess, but escaping to the backcountry only worked for so long. Sooner or later, Henry had to push himself out of his comfort zone.

But this was a lot more pushing than he'd expected.

If they had no chemistry or if he didn't feel safe, Henry wouldn't disclose to him, and it would just be any old awkward first date. It was that simple.

But if they did… then what would happen?

The butterflies were back in Henry's stomach as he zipped up his backpack and checked his watch for the fourth time that minute. He just had time for a quick shower and shave before he left for the airport.

As he opened the bathroom cabinet, Henry's gaze landed on the box of condoms on the shelf.

He bit his lip, half-reaching for them, hand hovering midair. Finally, he shook his head. "Fuck it," he muttered and grabbed them. He doubted he could click with anyone *that* much in just one date… but better safe than sorry.

Trying not to get his hopes up, he headed to the bedroom and jammed it into the backpack, then resumed his shave.

Despite his caution, Henry was excited at the prospect of a real date. He'd forgotten he *could* feel this excited. If worst came to worst and he didn't feel up to it, he didn't have to disclose to his date or do anything sexual. He could just make a new friend.

Rather than plunging in the deep end of dating, this could be a way of getting over his fear of the icy water and dabbling a toe.

But as he splashed water over his face and patted it dry, for the first time Henry allowed himself to admit that Trip was right. He did want and need more than he'd allowed himself to wish for in a long time.

Quite what he was supposed to do about it, Henry didn't know. But… one thing at a time. He had a flight to catch.

CHAPTER

Three

JADEN

"You're fucking kidding me. A plane?"

"Relax. Your therapist said you should push yourself, didn't she?" Despite his soothing words, Spence was clearly a touch worried himself. There was a wrinkle in his brow, and his grip on the steering wheel was tight.

Like Charon delivering a victim across the River Styx, he was driving Jaden to the airport. Meanwhile, Jaden was planning ways to shank him using only the contents of the glovebox.

If Jaden were thinking clearly, he might have agreed that he was ready for it. Logically, he knew it. After all, he'd been the one foolish enough to tell Spence he wanted to try leaving the house soon so he could start dating again.

Which had led to this whole escapade.

"I don't even know *who* I'm going on the date with." There was no way he could hide the fears that gripped him. What if the guy turned out to an asshole who laughed at him? And Jaden became this stranger's *weirdest first date* story for life?

"Relax. You're doubting my choice of date?"

"I seriously am," Jaden muttered under his breath, slumping back into the car seat.

As they pulled up in front of the departures entrance, Spence turned to him. "I'll have my phone on 24/7. So will your therapist."

"I know." Jaden wanted to believe Spence when he said he was there for him.

But he physically wouldn't be, and Jaden had to trust he was okay on his own for the date he'd won. They were flying to Phoenix, then taking a limo toward the Grand Canyon, stopping for a helicopter ride over it, and biking to a cabin for the night.

The thought of all that open air was making Jaden so nauseous he wanted to be sick.

Fuck, fuck, fuck.

"I can pull around—"

"Park here just to see me through security? No point. Save the parking fees." Jaden's voice was tight, but he offered a slight smile.

He *did* appreciate his brother helping, but goddamn, he could have used some more time to get used to the idea of going out before he actually did it. A week was not long enough to prepare. But right now, it felt like a lifetime wouldn't have been enough time, either.

Jaden switched his brain off. If he didn't think about this, it couldn't hurt him, right? He barely remembered checking in, or even the snaking security lines in the middle of the much too lofty atrium.

When he finally found his way to the gate, he clutched his backpack and tried to pretend it was a wall.

It didn't work very well.

A bright, cheery face appeared next to him. "Nervous flyer?"

Oh, God. "Nervous *liver*."

"As in liver of life, or liver that filters the alcohol out?"

It took Jaden a moment to come up with an answer to that. "At life. I'm a fucking chihuahua on a plane."

He buried his forehead in the knapsack and hoped this frankly gorgeous guy with the stubble (just long enough to be pettable, but not a real beard) and blue eyes (he'd always liked blue best) went away.

He was gorgeous—the most gorgeous man Jaden had laid eyes on in real life in *forever*—and no doubt full of perky energy. "Enough of these motherfucking chihuahuas on this… no, doesn't have the same ring," the stranger said.

Oh, man. He also had muscles. His t-shirt arms stretched around those biceps, and his pecs were clearly nuzzle-worthy. Even his lips looked kissable. In short, he was Jaden's type from head to toe.

Jaden snuck another look at the hottie, whose eyes twinkled with amusement. Belatedly, his gaydar started to ping. And he recognized those eyes. And the guy was flying to the same place as him…

He was getting an awful feeling about this.

"Are you on the Phoenix flight?"

"I am."

"For a blind date with a stranger?" It was the kind of question that either would be a yes or, hopefully, a confused "no" followed by the stranger backing away and leaving him to panic here in peace.

Luck was not on his side.

"I am."

"Fuck. Well, that's my first impression made." Jaden

buried his face in the backpack as his cheeks burned. *Great job, loser.*

"Don't worry about it. I'm Henry. Can I sit here?"

Jaden moaned and shrugged, wishing the floor would swallow him up.

Apparently Henry took that as a yes. He sat down and touched Jaden's shoulder. "You all right?"

"Aside from having just made the worst first impression ever on you, and the chance I'll projectile-vomit on the flight attendant, I'm awesome."

"Hi, Awesome. Got a last name to go with that?"

Damn it, the cutie was trying hard. It melted something of Jaden's defense mechanisms. He was used to people getting weirded out by him.

Then again, they were about to spend the next day together. May as well make it slightly less painful. The social equivalent of filing a broken nail after slamming his whole arm in a door. But even too little, too late would be better than sulking for the whole trip.

He gulped and looked up at last, focusing on Henry and not the expanse of the terminal behind him. "Jaden."

"Jaden," Henry repeated softly, and the smile that curved his lips was painfully attractive.

God, Henry was way out of Jaden's league. "Sorry. I think I'm your date."

Henry looked confused for a few moments, sticking out his lower lip in the most adorable way.

"Helicopter? Grand Canyon? Picnic in the great big vast outdoors?" Jaden prompted.

"Yeah. I've got that. Why apologize?"

Jaden just stared blankly at Henry. "I'm not... exactly... a hot commodity on the dating market."

Henry smiled and clapped his arm. "We all have our quirks. Or we wouldn't be choosing a date at a raffle, huh?"

"God. Don't tell me yours is that you're a serial killer. Or worse, serially optimistic." That smile was suspiciously bright even after Jaden had done his best to fuck up the introduction.

"Killing 'em with kindness? You could say that," Henry said, winking. "Guilty of at least one of the above."

"Do you tell me which in the helicopter?"

Despite himself, Jaden suddenly realized that he hadn't been nauseous in a few minutes. He had something—someone—to direct his attention toward.

His stomach had settled, and his brain had stopped whirling. Like he had tunnel vision, only now it was directed toward Henry and it was slowly expanding to include Henry within his bubble. He wasn't cured, far from it, yet the situation was now within his tolerance range.

Was that Henry's effect on him? There was something oddly trustworthy about his face. Probably a serial killer, Jaden decided.

They announced boarding, and Henry nudged him. "Here we go."

One way or another, he was getting out on a date.

With a hot, kind guy who only had a fifty-fifty chance of being a serial killer.

He was going to kill Spence, if he didn't fall in love first. What the hell? Anything could happen.

Henry had thought he was taking a pretty big leap out of his comfort zone. But as it turned out, Jaden was real, down-to-earth, and right now had a lot going on. Henry's fear of rejection felt like a footnote in comparison.

And… Jaden was super-cute. A couple inches shorter, he had a narrow face that tapered to a cute, pointed chin, light scruff along his jawline, golden-brown eyes, and full lips that curved up into a gorgeous smile.

All of which was incredibly distracting when Henry was trying to be a gentleman. The airplane seemed to be the easiest part of the journey for him, maybe because the plane was pretty small. Jaden had asked for the aisle seat so he didn't have to see the ground.

Henry had at first figured it was a fear of flying—a common fear, and a very sensible one, in his opinion. He preferred the ground himself. But it clearly wasn't just flying that Jaden was afraid of.

The conversation for the flight was easy. Henry stayed in work mode, calm and in control. He just chatted about TV shows, since he didn't want Jaden to ramble while he was nervous. Like alcohol, fear altered consciousness. It wouldn't be fair to exploit that.

By the time they landed, Jaden's anxiety had clearly ratcheted up again. Leaving the airport, he kept his head down and nearly sprinted to the limo that was taking them straight to the Grand Canyon.

At least it was just the two of them, so Henry could sit next to Jaden and keep his attention on something other than what was going on in his brain. Once they'd tossed their backpacks by their feet and buckled in, Henry settled back for the drive.

"What do you love doing? Tell me a bit about you," Henry encouraged with a smile.

It was an awkward first-date question, but on the other hand, talking about passions tended to bring people out of their heads. Henry knew that well from his own work guiding tourists through backcountry wilderness they might never have experienced before.

Jaden's gaze flickered to Henry's face, and then he fidgeted with his fingers, twisting them tightly together. "I love… um… I don't know. I used to love a lot of things, and then I got really depressed." He winced, clearly mortified. "Sorry."

Henry's heart squeezed with sympathy. He'd had his own years suffering under that fog. He knew exactly what it was like to drift away from things you once loved, until you felt like a stranger in your own life. He wanted to grab Jaden's hand and help bring him back into this moment, even just for today.

In his shoes, Henry wasn't sure he would have been able to go on a blind date in another state. That took balls.

"No need to apologize," Henry reassured Jaden easily. "Tell me anything you want."

They had a little while to drive, after all, and just the two of them to make conversation for the whole rest of the day—and tonight, and in the morning.

How the hell was he going to manage all of that? He hoped Jaden had more experience than him in managing an overnight date. Henry's last successful first date had been years ago, and that had led to a relationship, so he'd been off the market ever since.

And look how well that had gone. His stomach still flipped when he thought about trying to date again. And there was no escaping the fact this *was* a date.

Henry's heart raced, and he pushed his own anxiety back. There was nothing to lose, and everything to gain.

So far, he hadn't really gotten to know Jaden, but he already sensed that he was smart and funny when his anxiety wasn't taking over his adrenaline system. Surely he'd be open-minded, too.

Jaden gulped. "Right. So, I got depressed. Had to drop out of college, and I moved here—Denver, I mean—to get away from the memory of being such a loser."

It was hard for Henry not to interrupt and point out that Jaden was being a badass right now, no matter how much anxiety he had about it. He bit his lip to keep quiet and let Jaden talk.

"I live by myself now, in a little apartment with a mountain view. I work from home, doing phone-based jobs. They don't pay well, but it's something, at least. It's not a phobia of people, it's... agoraphobia, that's the technical term."

Henry glanced past Jaden at the wide-open, flat scrubland beyond and its pale dirt, tufts of scrubby bushes, mountains in the far distance. It had to be the worst place ever to bring an agoraphobe.

Open spaces scared Jaden? And he was going to the Grand Canyon? This was… a hell of a choice.

Henry wasn't sure he'd met anyone like Jaden before. The only way the poor guy could see nature was from his window, and Henry practically lived outdoors. How much more opposite could they get?

The way Jaden talked to him, like he wasn't sure which word came next, made it clear that he didn't hang out much with people face-to-face.

"What did you like before the depression spell?" Henry asked. He kept his tone gentle, trying to be as non-threatening as he could, since Jaden watched him like a deer in the headlights. He knew he had that effect on people sometimes since getting ripped.

Jaden paused. "Nobody asks me about that." He seemed taken aback, but not in a bad way—just curious now as he looked at Henry. "Why do you ask?"

"I used to be in therapy." Henry's throat felt tight as he thought of those sessions, trying to explain and justify who he really was, how long he'd known, and how sure he was. A very different kind of therapy, but still… he knew how it felt to be sure you were about to be abandoned. So he touched Jaden's arm. "Remembering the things that I felt passionate about helped me remember I was a real person behind the monsters in my brain."

And even though he'd just been vulnerable—not at all the tough guy people saw when they looked at him—Jaden didn't judge him for admitting his past. He just smiled at Henry slightly, letting out a breath. "Huh. Well, I used to like generic stuff… animals and walking outdoors. I never knew what I wanted to do. I was majoring in science, but I hadn't decided what field when I… yeah. Started my life as a hermit." His lip twitched with self-deprecating humor.

Henry filed those details away. "Really? You liked to spend time outdoors?"

"I loved it." Jaden sounded wistful as he drew a sigh.

"Well, I'm a wilderness guide, so…" Henry trailed off. Could he be the support Jaden needed to pick up one of his old hobbies? It was way too soon to tell.

"You are?" Jaden perked up. "Maybe someone knew what they were doing here."

"Fate?" Henry winked.

For the first time, he got a hint of adorable embarrassment from Jaden, like any old first date, even if they were really in a private car on their way to a helicopter ride and then a picnic. This was the most surreal first date of his life.

"Yeah," Jaden murmured, his cheeks flushed as he glanced anywhere else in the car but Henry. His smile was shy but hopeful.

"Well, my buddy Trip chose one for me. I was kinda torn between a few options, and he said he had a good idea…"

Jaden made a funny squeaking sound. "Trip? I met him. And my brother chose a raffle box on my behalf. Were you the one who wanted to talk to me?"

"Oh, my God." Henry covered his face, and it was his turn to blush. "How much did he tell you?" Trip had caught him trying to get a better look at Jaden after he'd come to his defense, and he'd just stormed over to play spy, before Henry could stop him.

Boy, was Henry glad that fate—in the form of their meddling friends—had intervened.

"Enough," Jaden winked, but then he grew distracted. "Are we going straight to the helicopter?"

Henry nodded. "I think that's the itinerary. But we can ask to change it." He was already figuring out who to call when Jaden put a hand on his knee.

"No. I'll be okay, I think. I just need to know what's coming so I can prepare for it."

Henry's skin lit up under his thin cotton walking trousers. He covered Jaden's hand with his own, wanting to provide comfort. It wasn't *just* comfort, though.

He suddenly couldn't look away from Jaden, their gazes locked. The sparks that ricocheted between them seemed to feed back into each other. In seconds, it was hard to breathe. All he wanted to do was slide his hand up Jaden's wrist to his forearm, and maybe his shoulder, and kiss him.

Fuck. He was pretty. It was impossible not to notice those wide, dark eyes framed by long lashes, and the full lips. Jaden looked like the twink next door, and he seemed almost too good to be true.

"So," Jaden said, his voice squeaking again, "what do you do? No, wait. You said. I mean, what does it involve?"

"Guiding?" Jaden nodded, and Henry squeezed his hand and smiled. "Mostly leading small groups. I do walking tours and backcountry guiding, though the latter tends to be for longer trips, up to a week or two."

"Yourself?"

"My own outfit? Nah, not yet. I'm working on it," Henry said with a confident smile. "I'm just about ready. Until now, I've been happy to hang back and keep… well, a steady job."

"Oh, that's understandable." Jaden seemed to be breathing better now, building his confidence.

"So you said your brother chose which raffle box to put your ticket into?" Henry prompted.

Jaden breathed out a quiet sigh, but the exasperation was affectionate as he rolled his eyes. "Yeah. We've always been pretty tight. He moved here to look after me."

Henry was a little less worried that Jaden was pushing himself way too far to meet someone else's expectations. He smiled. "Do you live with him?"

"Oh, God, no." Jaden laughed, his eyes wide with horror, which made Henry chuckle. "We thought about it, but we'd hate each other instantly. We get in each other's space too much."

It was hard to envision Jaden getting into anyone's space given how he'd spent half their time together so far shrinking back. But in the secure limits of his home, it made sense the real Jaden would come out. Henry drank in the knowledge eagerly.

"Oh, I see. Yeah. I've got a few sisters, and we..." Henry laughed quietly. "Yeah, did we ever fight growing up. About clothes, boys..."

The line never failed to get a grin, no matter what anyone knew about his history. Sure enough, it did the trick, and Jaden's lips curved up into another of those rare, beautiful little smiles.

"We still call each other to talk about stuff," Henry admitted freely. "Less about clothes, though."

"More about boys?"

Henry grimaced and shook his head. "Haven't had much time or energy."

"Hence putting your ticket into..." Jaden gestured around as if to indicate their date.

"You got it."

Jaden straightened up a bit and smiled. "So we're both new to this. I'm not the ugly duckling. That's good."

"You're not ugly at all," Henry answered instantly, his eyes wide at the very thought. Then he blushed. That had been pretty quick. At least Jaden knew he was interested, right?

Jaden was red, too. He mumbled, "Thanks. I think you're —I mean, you—you're hot," and stared out the window. He pressed a hand against his red cheeks, but he was smiling, too.

"Thanks." Henry grinned, his own confidence soaring. Oh, boy. He was going to have to watch his mouth. He could get himself into serious trouble with this cutie, and they still had a few hours to go in the limo.

This time, when Jaden put his hand on Henry's knee, Henry laced his fingers with Jaden's gently. He didn't say anything about it. He didn't need to. It was clear from their body language and expressions that this was new for them both—or at least, the first time in a long while.

And it felt good. No need to push it further until they were ready. They'd started opening up, and they had so much more time together.

Henry trusted Jaden already, enough to tell him more about himself. Jaden wasn't some alpha ad executive or suburban accountant with a trust fund. He'd been open and vulnerable, admitting he'd also been depressed, and Jaden hadn't shot him down.

Henry's fears were being put to rest, one by one, leaving him free to just enjoy himself like he hadn't taken time to do in a long time.

Maybe this was exactly what he'd needed.

CHAPTER
Five

JADEN

JADEN HAD JUST LEFT MILE-HIGH DENVER FOR THE FIRST TIME since he'd fled there and shut himself away in his house. Even the dry heat crept into the car, and he was positive he was loopy from the altitude change.

In one way, breaking out of his comfort zone this way was the most terrifying thing he could imagine, but in another… it was exhilarating. He wasn't rewatching Storage Wars for the eighth time.

The adrenaline crash would eventually come, and he knew he'd feel exhausted as shit, but he was going to enjoy himself here and now, goddamn it.

It was almost dizzying, letting go of his ideas about what he could do on a day to day basis. This was so far outside his everyday experience that his brain had stopped trying to dial the panic up. Now he just wanted to laugh hysterically, which was only slightly more fun than curling up in a ball.

He bit it all back and held Henry's hand tightly as they walked to the helicopter pad. The desert sun assaulted them once more, even in September. The amount of *sky* and *noth-*

ingness out there was hard to wrap his mind around. It was like walking the length of his living room ten times over just to get to the scraggly bushes on the edge of the launch pad. Helipad. Whatever the hell they called it. He'd tuned out most of the briefing.

"You doing okay?" Henry murmured in his ear.

Jaden liked that Henry was maybe four inches taller, but not a six-foot-something basketball player. None of that awkward stretching up to climb a fucking tree for a simple kiss.

Uh. Not that he was thinking about kissing him or anything.

"Fine," he squeaked, cursing his nervous habit. But Henry hadn't made fun of his voice warbling yet, and he just smiled at him.

"Good. Did you take in most of that briefing?"

Jaden guiltily shook his head. "Don't touch a moving blade, don't leap out?"

"That's about it," Henry agreed with a laugh before they reached the chopper and he effortlessly chatted with the pilot.

The small talk Henry did was still beyond Jaden. It felt like re-entering a whole social world he'd left behind, and not one toe at a time—a quick, icy plunge into the depths of Antarctic waters.

Henry seemed happy to do it, though. Much like Spence had been for the past few years, Henry was acting as a welcome buffer between Jaden and the world. Eventually, the pilot focused on things like starting the helicopter, so the chatter subsided.

Jaden stayed focused on his breathing and not how much of the world was out there, or who was seeing them hold hands, and what might happen as a result. At least Heart2-Heart had arranged the date, so the limo driver and pilot were clearly the accepting sort.

In an open area like this, PDA was scary, and he kept flinching at shadows. But the pressure of Henry's hand on his own helped Jaden's nerves, too. It was a confusing cycle of ups and downs in his brain.

It was stupid to try to explain, so he just clung on tight to the dark-haired, muscled hunk who was treating him so gently.

God, I have to fix my damage, Jaden thought. *But there's not a chance he'll stick around that long, will he?*

When they were seated, strapped in, and fitted with helmets that had built-in mics, his brain caught up with all that panic he hadn't gotten around to yet.

The white noise helped. It was a deafening din, and he could see the need for ear protection now. He was dimly aware of the helicopter rising, but tried to focus his attention on his own breathing. The sensation of the helicopter finding its balance in the air made his heart lurch into his throat.

But the whole time, Henry quietly held his hand and talked into his microphone about the Grand Canyon's unique natural environment. The pilot joked that he was usurping her job, so Henry asked if she could interrupt him whenever she needed to give her usual spiel. That way he could continuously talk in the downtime when she had to focus on flying.

"As long as Jaden's got something to focus on, we'll be good," Henry said.

"Oh, nervous flyer? They didn't mention it," she said.

Jaden tried to answer and say it was okay, but he was

speaking too softly for the microphone to pick up. He couldn't bring himself to make the half-shout that would be required. He resigned himself to communicating in gestures and expressions, which Henry had already proven adept at reading.

It took most of the flight before Jaden could finally bring himself to peek outside into the open air at the sights that Henry and their pilot—Shawna, he thought he'd heard—had been describing.

The canyon that yawned below him was… less terrifying than he'd expected. Sure, it was clearly huge, but the landscape was desolate and scarred deeply, and the human eye couldn't quite pick up a sense of scale. Without that, it might as well have been a toy landscape.

Red rocks towered from the canyon's floor and jutted out from the edges, and far below, what looked like a thin blue line of a river snaked along the bottom. It was kind of green down there, like there were trees.

Sure, the great outdoors was about a million times bigger than his safe little home in every dimension, but Jaden was still in that zone of giggly, lightheaded disbelief that he was actually living this and not dreaming.

He handled it fine until he spotted the shadow of the helicopter crossing a rock far below, tiny and dwarfed by its surroundings.

Poor Henry yelped as Jaden crushed his hand, choking on thin air. Jaden cursed and tried to loosen his grip, but he was pretty sure he was going to break the rail by his seat if he held it any harder.

"You okay?" Henry tried to hide his wince like a champ, even if Jaden saw through it.

Jaden just laughed and shrugged, letting his wild, wide

eyes tell the whole story. *Not really. This is too big. The helicopter isn't boxed in.* They were crunched into the backseat with a solid back behind them, but still, the sides were way too open to the air.

He checked out again, focusing on the grounding press of his body to the seat as his heart hammered. Time seemed to fly by without Jaden having much say in it. One moment they were up in the air, and the next he was listening to Henry and the pilot talk about the lives of coyotes as they landed, and then Henry was opening the car door for him.

Things had almost definitely happened in the meantime, like the helicopter landing, and maybe even the pair of them thanking the pilot. He had some vague idea he might have done that, but it was like the memory had just escaped as soon as the moment had passed.

That was the other reason he liked having Spence around —to tell him what he'd missed if he freaked out and it took him a while to calm down, and to handle other people while he did so.

Henry must have done that for him. Once more, Jaden's fear was interrupted by gratitude, because despite clearly having had to take charge of the situation, Henry wasn't looking annoyed or dismissive. He just cast Jaden little concerned glances as he helped him climb into the car, then came around the other side to join him.

Jaden's anxiety finally started to loosen its grip once they were inside the car, and he took a few deep breaths, leaning against the door.

This was good. He could handle this.

"Okay, wow."

"Back with me?" Henry smiled kindly and unlaced their fingers to click the buckle of his seatbelt before taking his hand again. "Buckle up and we'll get moving, hm? You're doing great. You're a star. I can't believe how much you've done today already."

God, Jaden hated himself. He wasn't the poster boy for Heart2Heart at all. If they wanted a cutesy story later, he'd have to tell them that Henry had needed to spend the whole date looking after him.

That was asking too much of anyone. That wasn't a date, it was a… lesson. In how to adult. God, he couldn't even do that, could he?

Jaden caught himself a few moments later. No, he always did this—beat himself up after a panic attack. He didn't deserve that.

I'm doing the best I can, he told himself firmly and straightened up. *Henry's choosing to support me when he doesn't have to. It's not like I'm forcing him. It's his choice—which makes it sweeter.*

"Where to?" Jaden managed, his fingers clumsy. Henry helped guide the metal buckle into place.

"Biking, just the two of us," Henry assured him. His deep voice rasped beautifully, and those bright blue eyes caught Jaden's gaze again. "With a picnic."

Jaden let out a deep breath. "Okay," he murmured. The thought of just the two of them, alone in the woods, was reassuring.

"And whatever you need to manage, we'll figure it out," Henry said with a smile.

Jaden's jaw dropped for a few seconds. He'd figured already that Henry was a considerate kind of guy, but this was more sensitivity and kindness than he'd ever expected. "I…" He teared up a little.

"Oh, hon." Henry unbuckled, ignoring the beep from the front seat of the limo, and slid the window to the front seats shut to block out the tutting sound from their driver—and give them privacy.

He buckled himself into the middle seat instead, suddenly so much closer.

It felt better, Jaden had to admit, to have Henry's arm around his shoulder instead of having to reach over the gulf of the middle seat between them.

Even if it dialed up the sparks between them to eleven. Henry was already distractingly hot. Being right next to him made Jaden's body ping with all kinds of good feelings.

Jaden swallowed a few more times, blinking back tears, and then smiled. "I'm being silly."

"No," Henry said softly. "I'm glad you're comfortable enough with me to express your feelings. I've got plenty of my own that people often can't handle."

That sounded like a distracting story. Jaden raised his eyebrows and did his best to look curious without prying.

Henry chuckled softly and put his hand on Jaden's knee again. It was quickly becoming their go-to thing. "Well," he hummed quietly. "I've been anxious about dating—about a lot of stuff—for a long time."

He rubbed his chin slowly, his gaze fixed on Jaden's face like he was assessing him. Henry was clearly running calculations that Jaden couldn't quite figure out. So Jaden stayed quiet and hoped Henry saw what he wanted in him.

Then Henry spoke up again, nodding firmly to himself as if he'd reached his decision. "I had to go to therapy, medically."

Another mystery, but not for long. Henry sighed quietly as if readying himself for an explanation.

Jaden knew the feeling. He'd pulled up a site on his phone about agoraphobia in case he had to explain it to his date. Henry hadn't needed the talk at all. He didn't come off like someone who had firsthand experience, but he'd clearly been in charge of people in the wilderness in extreme situations and had some kind of mental health training.

"Transition made dating kind of hard, or impossible. I wasn't sure if I should tell you, but it seems weird *not* to tell you," Henry admitted. "Especially after you've been so open."

Jaden blinked a few times and looked up at him. Transition? "You're... becoming... a woman?"

His mouth came out with the question before he really thought it through, and he blushed. There was probably so much wrong with his statement. Could he start again?

"No," Henry said, cracking a dry smile. "But thanks. Other way around."

Huh. Jaden hadn't even considered that as a possibility. Duh. Henry was big and buff and... well... not what he would have imagined from the stereotypes the media pushed forward.

Jaden had pretty much lived on YouTube for the last few years. He'd stumbled on videos here and there, enough that he knew some things, but clearly not enough to handle this situation with all the grace he could have hoped for. He was just gonna have to try his best.

"Sorry," Jaden said. "Good for you!" *Oh my God, that sounded dumb.* Jaden smacked his forehead with his palm, making Henry chuckle gently. "Maybe ignore that while I find my manners."

Henry laughed, a small but genuine sound. "It's a deal," he agreed.

Jaden nodded firmly. He didn't want Henry thinking he was a jerk about it. "I'm obviously kind of clueless. Maybe we can chat about it while we're biking?" Jaden quickly offered, hoping to make up for it before he hurt Henry.

But Henry didn't look angry. If anything, Henry's smile was cautiously hopeful. "If you've got questions, yeah. I don't let just anyone quiz me, but I don't mind if you do. And I'm proud of being trans. I've never been ashamed of it. It's just part of me. It's made me who I am."

Jaden nodded. "I know what you mean."

He sure as hell wouldn't be the same person if it weren't for these last few years of his life. In some ways, they'd been hellish, but he was clawing his way up from that pit. Enough that he could appreciate where he was now.

A year ago, he wouldn't have even dreamed of coming on this date. But he was here, and he was even enjoying himself despite the anxiety that had tried to gnaw at him. On the other side of all that fear was… where he was. Still here with a cute guy who was patiently smiling at him.

Safe and sound.

What doesn't kill you makes you stronger was a slogan he hated with a passion—but for better or for worse, his struggles over the last few years had definitely shaped him.

"I'm glad we're both here," Henry said with such conviction that it made Jaden sit up just a bit straighter.

He felt just a little more normal.

Was it such a bad thing to want that? With Henry here, holding his hand both literally and emotionally, Jaden was starting to think it wasn't a bad thing—and it wasn't out of reach.

He had to take risks in therapy to get anywhere. What if it was the same in life?

Jaden could only hope.

CHAPTER
Six

HENRY

They'd parked their bicycles, taken off the picnic baskets on the front of each bike, and unloaded the food and drinks. The clearing was already decorated, lit LED lamps hanging around it and blankets spread. A little sign stuck into the ground had the H2H logo and their names printed on it, confirming they'd gotten to the right place.

Around them, trails snaked around trees, and the parkland felt open and surprisingly quiet. The underbrush was low and scrubby, but shade-loving desert wildflowers were here, too.

It was the perfect chance to really talk to each other. They'd already made the usual boring small talk in the car on the way from the airport, and up in the helicopter. There wasn't much left in the way of shallow get-to-know-each-other games.

Henry felt safe enough with Jaden to talk about his own past, present, and… well, future.

Jaden was leagues ahead of most guys Henry had tried to talk to already.

Years of transition had taught Henry how to deflect questions—not how to soften the blows that inevitably lay within innocent questions. He would have to absorb some hits from unintended ignorance.

But Jaden was clearly kind and meant no harm, so he was off to a good start. Henry was willing to be patient and take a chance on him.

And it was a beautiful setting to stop and relax. The trees were tall, elegant Ponderosa pines and oaks. The dirt was still the distinctive rusty red of the canyon, but elderberry, broad-leafed shrubs, and tufted grasses filled the spaces between the trees.

"Want some lemonade?" Jaden asked, smiling brightly at Henry. He'd relaxed since they'd entered the woods. With less open space around them, Jaden came alive, his eyes bright and smile eager.

"Yes, thanks," Henry answered, settling on the picnic basket to accept the drink. Was now a good moment to talk? They had food and drinks to enjoy, and nothing else to distract them.

As if reading his mind, Jaden spoke up. "Can I talk a bit?"

"Of course."

As they took in the scenery and Henry noted the very different plant life, Jaden talked in that quiet, lilting voice about his past. He'd been in college, like he'd said before. As for the incident that prompted him to leave SoCal and come all the way out to Denver, Henry was sad to hear that he'd privately guessed right.

"I got nearly beaten up for looking a little too gay. The Santa Monica boardwalk, of all places."

Henry's eyes widened. He was planning on going there in

just a few weeks! Should he tell him? No, definitely not the moment.

Jaden saw him stare. "I know. But…" Jaden trailed off with a miserable shrug. "They didn't care where they were. They hit my boyfriend instead of me. We broke up a couple weeks later. He moved out of the state, and he's never talked to me again. You know how in all those videos about gay guys who've been attacked, they say they're stronger now? What if you're not? What if you just crumbled?"

He wasn't crying, though his voice wavered. He cast little glances around the clearing and up to Henry as he talked.

Jesus, Henry wished he could have been there to protect and support Jaden. It was suddenly hard to breathe. All he wanted to do now was sweep Jaden into the world's tightest hug.

And never let anyone harm a hair on his head again.

Henry scooted closer, putting an arm around Jaden's shoulders. He swallowed back his anger and grief and frustration as he nodded. "And that's what you feel like you did? Crumble?"

"Well, I stopped leaving the house," Jaden mumbled. "And I ran away, too."

"But you're out here now," Henry told him, soft and admiring. "Maybe you needed that time to rebuild yourself."

Jaden nodded. "I'm working on it. I'm getting a service dog really soon, actually." He brightened up just a little. "I want to be able to go get my own groceries. That's the goal. But I'm not there yet. Barely keeping it together today."

"I can tell," Henry admitted. The strain it was taking on Jaden was obvious. "But you're doing so damn well."

"It's just because I've gone through so much panic that my

panic button has broken and I'm stuck in *is this reality or a dream* mode." Jaden managed a smile.

"But you haven't turned tail and run away," Henry urged, wanting Jaden to think better of himself.

Jaden cast him a small smile, then cleared his throat. "And you're getting out into... the dating world. So that's something to be proud of."

"I'm just glad you didn't immediately go *ew, get away from me,*" Henry admitted with a breathy laugh to cover up the jolt in his stomach. The self-deprecation had hit a little too close to home.

Sure, Henry was about as okay with himself as anyone was with themselves. More than that—he felt blessed to be at home in his body now. That didn't stop others' reactions from stinging.

His palms were sweaty as he gripped his glass of lemonade tightly.

"Of course not. I don't understand a lot, but I know some things from the internet," Jaden told him. "I don't want to hurt you with dumb questions, though."

"You can ask anything," Henry told him, then smiled. "If it's rude, I'll tell you." He dabbed his forehead with his sleeve, trying to settle his nerves.

"O-Okay, good." Jaden shot him a wry look. "Is surgery the first thing everyone asks about?"

Henry snorted with bitter amusement. "Yeah. Like they're only trying to figure out if they'd fuck me, without bothering to ask if *I* want to fuck *them.*"

"I wouldn't even think to ask that yet," Jaden admitted. "I wasn't looking for a quick hookup. I wanted to see where this date goes. But I *do* think you're super hot," he added, laughing sheepishly.

Henry blushed and grinned, his heart swelling with pride. "Yeah? So are you. I thought you were super cute in the terminal. I was really hoping you were my date. Thank God you were, or some random dude would be really weirded out."

Jaden giggled. "So… if dysphoria is a problem, you can tell me what you feel comfortable with. Or just tell me what you want and when you want it. I'm easy to please." He flicked a shy little smile over at Henry.

Oh, God. He was being so adorable right now. If Henry read him right, he was *begging* to be on the bottom. "Yeah?" Henry said. "If it gets to that, I'm a top. In case that's a surprise. A lot of guys are surprised."

Jaden shook his head. "I don't know what confuses them. You've been *radiating* big dick energy all day," he said, laughing.

Henry grinned at him, surprised at the strength of the relief that swept through him. "I hate to brag, but… I love to brag." Talking about this was so much less awkward than he'd feared.

Jaden giggled. "So, I'm pansexual," he said, glancing at Henry. "If you know what that is…"

Henry smiled fondly as memories flooded back to him. "Yeah. I'm gay, but I know what pan is. When I learned about it online, they used to call it *hearts, not parts*."

"Oh?" Jaden blinked at him. "I don't really like that phrase. It's not necessarily about parts for bi people. But people's gender is never a factor in my crushes, so I say pan instead of bi."

"Right," Henry nodded. "I know more about it now, but I'm glad I found that phrase. It helped me a lot back then. Changed my life, even."

Jaden shifted to grab the bottle of lemonade and top up their glasses. "How so?"

Henry sipped his drink and tried to come up with the right words. "Back when I started transitioning, I thought what a lot of people do: that only pan people date trans people."

"Oh," Jaden murmured. "But that can't be right."

Henry laughed. "Yeah. It's bullshit, but that's where my brain was at. I figured gay guys wouldn't be into me, and I obviously didn't want to date straight guys. And I thought bi guys wanted either men or women, and they wouldn't want someone 'in-between.' When you're just coming out, you're still wrestling with all kinds of crap the world puts on you. Even back then, *I* knew I was a man whether or not other people saw me that way. But I didn't want to get turned down. Even if it was because of their hangups, I was the one who'd have to deal with the fallout."

Jaden nodded, running his hand gently along Henry's arm. "Gotcha," he murmured.

Henry swallowed hard. It hurt to think how many barriers he'd flung up for himself. "Basically, I thought my dating life was over until I'd had surgery. And even then, I was scared. What if surgery went wrong? What if I didn't end up with something that made people think *ah yes, of course that's a guy*? I pretty much thought nobody would ever find me attractive again."

Ouch. The words had just fallen out without even thinking about them, and his throat was suddenly tight.

"Oh, hon," Jaden breathed out sympathetically, and the pet name actually felt... *good*. He said nothing more, just frowned like he was waiting for Henry to continue.

"And then I stumbled on that phrase and the existence of

pan people. And I thought... well, for the first time, I had hope. That maybe my parts wouldn't matter to someone, if I found the right someone. That it was about what was in my heart."

"Did you?" Jaden asked, his soft voice hard to hear.

"Turns out a lot of people like hearts, not parts—not just pan people. When I finally got up the courage, I ended up dating a gay guy. But he liked my parts, too. Especially that he could choose his own adventure." Jaden stared blankly at him, so Henry smirked. "Size-wise."

"Oh. *Oh!*" Jaden turned an adorable shade of red but he giggled hard. "Oh, my God."

Henry laughed. "So yeah, you don't have to be pan—or even bi—to like trans guys. Who knew?" Henry smiled softly. "But the idea that there'd still be someone out there for me... that made all the difference."

He didn't often think about those early years, between starting testosterone and top surgery and finally finding a way to get bottom surgery.

"But you broke up?" Jaden continued after a few moments of silence.

"Yeah." Henry sighed. "We were never really on the same page outside the bedroom. After him, I dated another gay guy for a while. But he was too impatient to wait for me to be..." He grimaced, his chest twisting at the memory. "Done. *Complete*, he said."

"With... transition? Medically?" Jaden asked, shaking his head softly. He reached out to touch Henry's arm. "Sorry. I know I'm being dumb here."

Jaden was keeping up pretty well, all things considered. Henry smiled slightly at him. He could have said a lot worse. His ex's words had just played into Henry's own fears, and reliving that was hard. He was fucking complete all on his own, thanks very much.

"No, it's fine. Bottom surgery has a couple stages. Until I was all done, I couldn't get hard." He tried to speak clinically so he wouldn't get distracted, but looking at those beautiful pools of brown eyes made him flush with that excited embarrassment. "I couldn't just, um… fuck him on the spot like he wanted me to." The sting was still fresh in his chest when he spoke those words. "So he dumped me." Henry's voice was more raw than he'd expected.

"Ouch," Jaden murmured. His eyes were wide and shining with wetness. He pressed into Henry's side and slid his arms around his waist in a gentle hug. "Jesus. Even if you're not trans, that would hurt any guy to hear. That must have been awful for you."

"It was. It made my dysphoria go nuts." Henry looped his arms around Jaden's shoulders to hug him for a few moments as his chest flooded with that shame all over again. "It was frustrating for him, sure. But it was so much worse for me. It's impossible to describe what it's like when your instincts are screaming at you to do something your body just… won't allow."

"Ah, man," Jaden murmured. "I don't know what that's like. But I do in another way. I know how hard it is to fight my brain."

Henry swallowed hard and nodded. "So… yeah. I've come a long way. But in some ways, I'm still kind of afraid that people won't like my heart *or* my parts, whether or not they're pan." He tried to bring the conversation back around, giving Jaden a breathy laugh.

The fresh air breezing over his face helped ground him,

reminding him that he wasn't there anymore. He wasn't that guy anymore, either. Not just physically, but mentally.

He felt light, yet strong. His vulnerability had only brought them closer, and Jaden was pressed against him, sharing comfort. Trusting him had been the right choice, and Henry couldn't stop smiling.

Jaden finally pulled away from the hug and opened the picnic basket. "I haven't dated trans people before, but that's just because… um, I don't really date, like I said." He laughed sheepishly. "But I want to."

Henry had to swallow back his eagerness in order to think straight. Or, not-at-all straight. "Yeah?"

"Yeah. So… thank you for telling me all of that." Jaden smiled and offered him a napkin.

Henry chuckled and accepted it. "You're welcome. Thank you for listening. Didn't expect to get so much off my chest."

He was hungry now, and he felt great. These things had been locked away for far too long, like rust gnawing at the secret corners of his heart. Getting them into the open air made his spirit feel brighter.

It was all so sudden, but sudden didn't mean it couldn't be profound. Just like a change in the weather could leave the landscape forever altered, Henry was gonna catch this man, whatever it took.

"Which way will sunset be?"

Henry squinted around, just to show off a little, before pointing to the sky over a corner of the clearing. "Should be around there."

If only he knew the area, he could have impressed Jaden by gathering mushrooms to add to their picnic. Foraging, another of his hobbies, was usually seen as kind of eccentric, but Jaden had taken well to everything else.

Probably better not to risk poisoning him on the first date in an unfamiliar biome. Henry shook his head and shelved the thought. He had to save up his impressive talents and deploy them strategically.

Jaden beamed. "Probably a real-life guide and not a serial killer, then." His laugh startled even Henry, who grinned.

"I solemnly swear not to serial-kill you. Well, I suppose it would be a single kill. That's not very exciting."

Jaden grinned. "I wanna make a *le petit mort* reference, but that's probably inappropriate."

The little death—it meant orgasm in French, Henry knew. His heart skipped a beat, and suddenly the warm heat of Jaden pressing into him was awakening the cravings he'd long ago set aside.

Ignoring this would be difficult—and he wasn't sure he wanted to. The prickles of heat along his skin made him crave skin contact like nothing else.

"I want to kiss you."

"Please," Jaden whispered, turning his face toward Henry.

It was all the invitation Henry needed to press their lips together and finally get a taste of the cutie who had been captivating him all day.

Their kiss was warm and sweet and slow. Their lips slid together as they tasted and explored, the first sparks shooting through them.

Jaden's lips were so soft and precious, and he clung to Henry's chest and stayed perfectly still, like he was waiting for Henry to take the lead.

It only came naturally to do so. Henry wanted to kiss him until he left him gasping, and then treat him to a night that he'd never forget. He growled under his breath and sucked

Jaden's lower lip, but it just made Jaden giggle softly against his mouth.

How fucking precious he was, and he didn't even know it.

The kisses quickly deepened, and before long, they were gasping into each other's mouths, hands roaming up and down backs and arms and shoulders.

"You're really…" Jaden trailed off, sounding hoarse, when they finally pulled apart. "Hot. God. You make me forget words."

Henry grinned. "Thanks," he teased. "I'll take that as a compliment."

"Very compliment, yes."

That made Henry giggle, which made Jaden dissolve in a fit of laughter of his own. They both flopped onto their backs and gazed up at the sky.

It took Henry a second to remember that it might make Jaden nervous to see that much open air, but when he looked over, Jaden had his eyes closed and a smile on his face. He looked giddily contented, if that were even a thing—satisfied, yet almost childishly pleased with himself.

Frankly, it was adorable.

Henry chuckled and sat up to rummage through their picnic foods, setting out the spread on the other blanket.

"What if I'm too tired to sit up?" Jaden complained from the ground.

Henry grinned as he plucked a grape off the stem. "I can deal with that. Open up."

Jaden's eyes flew open. When Henry pressed the grape against his lips, he bit it and mumbled, "Not where I thought that was going."

They both dissolved into laughter again.

Yeah. Today was going just fine by any standards. Maybe, just maybe, this could work out as more than one date.

He tried to ignore how desperately he wanted it to and tell himself *only if it's right,* but he couldn't shake the instinct that told him that of course this was right. It already felt strangely like they'd known each other for years.

"You know, we're not in a rush today," Henry said slowly. "We *do* live in the same city. We can see each other again."

Jaden's eyes cracked open as he looked over at him. The hope on his face was undeniable. "You want to? I'm not too… weird?" He sounded surprised.

"Of course," Henry breathed out, widening his eyes in surprise that Jaden was even asking the question. "Duh. Oh my God, duh."

That sent Jaden into another blushing fit that made him cover his face, but he was beaming too hard to hide. "Then yeah, we could hang out sometimes. I don't have any friends, really. That would be nice."

Henry's chest swelled with excited anticipation, even if it was tempered by Jaden's statement. Seeing Jaden again wasn't *all* he wanted. He either hadn't quite understood what Henry was suggesting, or he wasn't interested. And Henry was almost positive it was the first, not the second.

Maybe Henry was the crazy one for even thinking of it, after knowing each other for just one afternoon so far. But… there was no mistaking what his heart wanted.

Just see how tonight goes, he told himself. They could make it work back in Denver. He was sure of it. Jaden was worth the work. That just left one thing: asking him out, properly, for a second date… before the first date was even over.

That conversation could wait until after supper.

CHAPTER
Seven

JADEN

As afternoon drew to a close, the first sign of evening creeping up on Henry and Jaden was the chill in the breeze. They'd each shrugged on extra layers as the scorching daytime heat faded.

The lamplit picnic area was perfectly serene and romantic, and nobody had interrupted them.

Watching Henry's effortless confidence reading a map and compass to get them here on their bikes had been so hot. Jaden had always wanted the confidence to navigate, but he'd never gotten that far in his outdoor pursuits. Back in college, he'd gone on trail runs. That was as wild as it got.

But Henry did *real* wilderness shit. This must be nothing to him. Jaden found himself letting Henry lead the way, and he actually enjoyed it.

Their supper had been delicious—fried chicken, potato salad, a bottle of sparkling wine, all the classic picnic foods. Now Jaden and Henry were lying together, waiting for…

For what, Jaden wasn't quite sure.

Their cabin was nearby, Henry said. They could bike to it

in minutes, even at a gentle pace. For now, they were digesting supper, talking about anything and everything, and admiring the changing colors of the sky.

The breeze rustled through the trees, and being in these woods felt strangely home-like. This was freedom in a way Jaden wasn't quite sure he was ready to handle, but had been craving for years.

"I'm so glad I did this," he whispered.

Henry took his hand. "Me too. I wish we could stay out here and stargaze… but biking in the dark would be quite a life choice."

"Yeah," Jaden laughed. He didn't want to leave the clearing just yet. He had one thing left to do first. "We've got a few more minutes?" he asked Henry.

Henry frowned, glancing at the fading light, but Jaden widened his eyes with his plea. Henry relented into a smile and laughed. "A few minutes," he echoed.

"Thank you." Jaden squeezed his hand. "I'm just… enjoying this."

A rush of breath left Henry's lungs, and he looked over. "Yeah?"

At the same moment, Jaden had looked at him. That brought their lips just inches apart as they gazed into each other's eyes.

Henry was gorgeous: stubbly, gorgeous, rugged. The kind of guy who had tons of followers on Instagram. His jaw was square and handsome, and his lips were thin but very kissable. And best of all were his bright blue eyes, a shade that stood out even in the dimming light.

Jaden wanted a piece of that, more than he was willing to admit.

"Hm?" Henry prompted, but he was smiling slowly. There was wicked temptation in that smile.

Jaden gave up resisting and leaned in to press their lips together.

It was warm and comforting, slow and thick as molasses. Which was what Jaden's mind felt like as he sank into the sweet kiss. It started as a gentle exploration, but more swelled between them quickly.

So to speak.

Jaden gulped, his cheeks burning as he grew hard. He savored the taste of Henry; the smell of him, spicy and sweet; the warmth of his thigh pressing into Jaden's knee.

Henry shifted, resting his hand on Jaden's upper arm as he kissed him, sucking his lip gently. His stubble prickled at Jaden's smooth cheeks whenever he caught his breath. As their kiss went on, Henry slowly ran his hand around to the back of Jaden's neck.

Henry's confidence sparked something deep inside Jaden. It made him feel at home somehow. Comfortable in his presence, and even curious. Did Henry want to relax and let someone else take over, even for a bit?

Jaden was desperate to show Henry how turned on he was—to take charge for just a minute. The boldness grew to an insatiable hunger, and he finally couldn't resist.

Jaden shifted until he propped himself up on his elbows, half-straddling Henry with his shoulders only. Henry's eyes were half-lidded as he stared up, his breathing heavy as a smile touched his lips. The unfiltered desire in his gaze made it very clear that he was okay to continue, so Jaden pressed a kiss against Henry's mouth.

Henry grabbed the back of Jaden's head and deepened the kiss, his teeth grazing along Jaden's lips until they stirred

Jaden's blood into a dull roar. He tingled with the need for more.

All that mattered right now was the two of them.

Jaden ran a hand down Henry's chest and pulled back from the kiss with a small wet sound. When Henry tried to sit up, Jaden pressed him back down with a hand against that firm brick wall of a chest. Then he winked.

Henry smiled and yielded, rolling his head back to bare his throat and the sensitive skin of his neck. Jaden dove closer, pressing gentle kisses and licks.

What would it be like to do it right here? Jaden's heart pounded at the very thought. But… no, he'd wait for the cabin. The anticipation would make it all the better. Jaden wanted to turn Henry on and leave him wanting more, until he couldn't resist jumping him the moment they got through the door.

God, he was ready to go further with Henry. It felt right— so right he couldn't possibly explain it, even to himself. Jaden wanted to be irresistible and spontaneous, for the first time in what felt like forever.

Henry's quiet moans slipped through the night air as Jaden kissed his pulse point and throat, licking down to his collarbone and nibbling gently.

He wanted to haul up Henry's shirt and keep going, lavishing kisses on the rippling muscles he glimpsed under the thin material. But that was a little too bold, even for him.

"Are you trying to drive me crazy?" Henry breathed out, his voice hoarse. He kneaded Jaden's shoulders, nails digging in through Jaden's thin sweater.

"Nooo," Jaden giggled. He just wanted to get Henry in the mood—not so hot that the bike ride would be uncomfortable, but enough to tempt him into doing something more tonight than talking over coffee.

"I think that's a yes," Henry breathed out.

Jaden pulled back and smirked. "It's definitely a yes." Oh, man. *He* was gonna be the one with the awkward boner during the bike ride. He adjusted himself with a nervous giggle.

"Wow," Henry whispered when Jaden pulled back. He stretched, arms above his head, and then rubbed his face as he rolled onto his side to face Jaden. "Well, I liked that."

Jaden grinned, walking his fingers down Henry's chest. "Yeah?"

Henry nodded hard. "Whatever you're looking for—that worked."

"I was worried," Jaden admitted, "that you wouldn't feel up to sex. Since you said you're still exploring things…"

Henry chuckled deeply. "That was then. This is now." He stroked Jaden's cheek gently, the pad of his thumb catching against the stubble along Jaden's jaw. "And you're turning me on like crazy."

Jaden giggled with the sheer relief and excitement. Tonight was going in all the right directions. "My sex drive isn't usually that high. But you make me feel…" he trailed off and shook his head.

How to describe the intoxication that filtered through his veins at the slightest brush of Henry's fingers along his skin?

"Good. I was prepared to just cuddle tonight," Henry said with a grin, in a tone that made it clear he was on the same page.

Should Jaden admit it? Yes, of course. Henry wasn't going to shame him for it, and if he did, they weren't well-matched anyway. "That's what I miss the most about relationships—just cuddling."

Henry nodded. "Yeah. Yeah, I missed it, too." He was absentmindedly stroking Jaden's arm, those long fingers playing with his shirt like he didn't even know he was doing it.

"I cuddled with my friends in college," Jaden admitted, laughing. "People thought I was dating everyone. But I'm just tactile."

He'd almost forgotten that about himself. Not many people visited him now, and it wasn't so normal to just crash for naps with people or share a room if they were out partying late. Plus, gay guys got the wrong idea if he grabbed them to cuddle.

Not that that was always bad, but not every hard-on had to be indulged. His current one disagreed, but he ignored Jay Junior. He was not going to screw up this wonderful date by doing the wrong thing.

"We should probably bike back to the cabin now," Jaden said, his voice deep and low with meaning. He tried for flirtatious bedroom eyes. "And also, it's getting dark and we'll crash our bikes."

Henry's eyes widened and he sat up, then laughed. "Yeah. I hardly noticed."

"Did I distract you?" Jaden stood up and looked at the mess.

"They'll be by to clean up for us in, uh… twenty minutes," Henry told him after checking his watch, waving a hand. "Glad you nudged me to check the time. That might have been awkward."

"It would have been more awkward if we'd done what *I*

was thinking about," Jaden murmured boldly, grinning when Henry's eyes went wide.

"Come on. Let's go," Henry said, sliding his arm around Jaden's shoulders. His steps were quick and purposeful, making Jaden laugh.

"Is the cabin already set up?" Jaden had left his backpack in the limo along with Henry's. Whoever was arranging things here was supposed to have dropped them off for them.

"Yep. Well, we can only hope," Henry chuckled. "Let's go."

The last part of their ride seemed to pass in the blink of an eye, but not the way the helicopter ride had terrified him for so many minutes that it was hard to tell them apart. Instead, the sense of peace that had settled into his spirit made Jaden sleepy and happy.

Once they pulled up in front of the little place, it was unmistakable—there was a sign on the door with their initials and "H2H."

No rainbow flags or names on the door. Jaden appreciated the touch of discreetness, even if they hadn't bumped into anyone else. It wasn't like they were *really* in danger, he reminded himself once again. Not here, in the wilderness, alone together.

The dark wooden cabin had a little porch in the front and small windows facing the road. Jaden caught just a glimpse of a much larger window along the side of the cabin, blinds currently drawn across it. In the morning, that would be a wonderful view of the forest wildlife.

Jaden and Henry left their bikes outside and headed into the place. It might be new ground, but it felt nice and safe instantly. With walls around him, Jaden was more confident and bold. He was the first inside, and the first to find the single bedroom with its huge king bed.

"I'll take the couch—" they both started to say when they stood in the doorway, looking down at it.

Then Jaden giggled under his breath. The air practically buzzed between them, so he reached out to take Henry's hand, his own body sparking with pleasure at that simple contact. "Together?" he murmured. "At least to start with."

Henry nodded jerkily. "That's… that would be nice." For the first time, he sounded nervous, and he was smiling sheepishly. "Is there anything in the fridge?"

"Let's see," Jaden said simply. He followed Henry to the kitchen, shoving his hands in his pockets and leaning on the little countertop as he watched him.

Was he nervous about spending the night together? Jaden was excited at the idea, but he could see how Henry might feel vulnerable. They *had* only met that morning. It felt longer, like they'd spent several dates together already.

"If you don't wanna cuddle—or do anything more—I won't take it personally. We hardly know each other yet. I really don't mind the couch," Jaden murmured, reaching out to touch his arm.

Henry swallowed hard as he pulled out glasses and poured water for them both. "Yeah…" he trailed off, sounding uncertain. Then, he shook his head. "But no. I want more. I just don't want to rush into this and screw this up."

"Oh, believe me," Jaden laughed. "Me neither. But things are going fine. When we're overthinking it less and kissing more, I'd even say *great.*"

Henry gave him a small, grateful smile. "Before I met you, I figured I'd take things slow. I didn't even know if I was going to out myself. And now… it's just hit me how fast all of this is."

Jaden nodded and stepped aside so he could close the fridge again. "Too fast?"

"No," Henry said, smiling at him. "Not at all. I guess I didn't know what to expect."

The energy that jolted through Jaden's skin when Henry passed him the glass of water made him shiver from head to toe. Just his knuckles brushing against his skin made him wonder what it would be like to have those fingers brushing against *other* sensitive parts—his cock, which was still half-hard and hopeful, or his nipples.

God, anywhere. Henry could tease him for hours on end and Jaden wouldn't even cry about it. He felt so *alive* right now, it was impossible to describe.

"Fuck," Jaden whispered under his breath and smiled to himself as he shook his head. Yeah, Henry was right. He hadn't expected to connect with his date *this* quickly.

Let alone to find himself raring to explore more. He didn't know what Henry had going on in his pants, but whatever it was, Jaden just wanted to make him feel good. He'd learn how, if he had to.

"You okay?" Henry instantly asked, concern flickering over his face.

Jaden just smiled faintly at him and shook his head. "More than all right. Come on. Let's get changed into PJs and talk, hm?"

Henry relaxed and smiled at him. "Yeah. That sounds good." He set down his water glass and grabbed the backpack waiting by the door, then headed for the bathroom.

While he was in there, Jaden hastily got changed himself and then slid onto the bed. He sat on the bedspread in the strange bedroom, his whole body thrumming with nervous anticipation.

Whatever ended up happening between them, Jaden couldn't wait for it. But one thing was for sure: this wasn't anything like he'd expected. *Henry* wasn't anything like he'd expected. And he was so glad.

Now, if he could figure out what was on Henry's mind, all of Jaden's worries would be vanquished for at least a few blissful hours.

"Comfy?" Jaden's lips curved up in a small, hopeful smile as he gazed over—and a few inches up—at Henry. He looked worried. Bless him, he was trying his best to make Henry feel more comfortable.

"Yeah," Henry murmured, grateful that Jaden hadn't gotten grouchy at him when he'd suddenly pulled back. He didn't even feel like he needed to explain himself. Jaden was smart enough to put two and two together and realize that Henry was out of his depth. "I'm okay."

He was still nervous about what Jaden might say or do, but he was excited, too. Like he'd graduated from climbing boulders to climbing cliffs. He was plunging head-first toward something he couldn't quite escape. And he didn't *want* to escape it. He wanted to embrace this new reality they were crashing into, and let it sweep him away.

He just hoped Jaden didn't react in discomfort or, worse, disgust. The sight of someone recoiling at his body—that brought back memories that he fought away. *Jaden's different,* he thought, more prayer than certainty. *I have to give this a chance.*

"Okay, good," Jaden murmured back, fidgeting with the buttons on his silky blue PJs. Henry felt underdressed in his plaid PJ bottoms and plain white T-shirt.

They were on top of the bedcovers, rearranging pillows. By unspoken mutual agreement, neither of them had pulled back the covers yet. Surely that meant they both had the same thing on their minds.

"Look, I... I haven't had sex since my last operation," Henry admitted quietly. "I've still been getting to know how my body works," he admitted with a breathy laugh. "But I want you. So I'm struggling to figure out what to do next."

Jaden licked his lips, his gaze unmistakably wandering along Henry's body until Henry prickled with pleasure. "I want you, too. So kiss me."

And Henry did. Their lips slid together in a burst of pleasant warmth that made him tingle from head to toe. "That's a good start. I'm up for this anytime."

"Noted." Jaden's breathing was heavy, and his voice did that adorable squeaking thing again.

Henry grinned. "I want to enjoy tonight. It feels like we've known each other forever."

"It *has* been a long day," Jaden laughed. "I spent it holding your hand. Crushing, more like."

"It wasn't a hardship," Henry teased. His palm still tingled at the memory of Jaden's hand laced with his. It made him feel like Jaden's protector—strong and foolishly smitten.

He eased himself onto his back, gazing at Jaden. Just as he'd hoped, Jaden turned onto his side and scooted closer, his gaze wide and shy. His hand came to rest tentatively in the middle of Henry's chest.

Henry covered it with his own for a moment, reassuring him with a smile that this was okay. More than okay: his nerves came alive. With just a thin t-shirt in the way, his skin was suddenly warm. He itched for that hand to start roaming.

No sooner had he thought it than Jaden started rubbing across his flat chest, starting in small circles that awakened and excited him. Until, of course, Jaden's thumb wandered up and caressed the peaks of his nipples.

Jaden caught his breath, his gaze flickering up like he was waiting for a reaction. Henry didn't want to disappoint Jaden, but he wasn't going to fake it, either.

He couldn't feel the touch there, but it wasn't unpleasant, at least. Jaden *was* turning Henry on. He loved the sight of Jaden's thumb lifting over the small peaks of his nipples, poking against his shirt. Watching that hand glide smoothly across his chest fascinated Henry endlessly.

The smallest moments could be the most erotic. Could he ever explain to Jaden what trade-offs he'd chosen, and why? Feelings didn't translate to words well. There was no way to describe that gnawing void he'd once felt, and how its conspicuous absence magnified the pleasure Henry felt.

"I want to make you feel good," Jaden murmured. "What do you like?"

Henry's heart thumped, and his chest tightened with nerves. This part wasn't easy for anyone, but in the past, it had been especially uncomfortable—even risky—for him. "I've had… well, it's easier to show you. Is that all right?" He didn't want to spend all night explaining when he could just cut to the chase.

"If we're getting naked, let me start, then." Jaden gave him a warm smile and unbuttoned his pajama top, making eye contact as he did so. The ends of the fabric grazed Henry's stomach as Jaden revealed his slender, smooth chest one button at a time.

His frame was lean and narrow, easily dwarfed by Henry's. He was fascinating and precious, and just a little bit breakable.

God, his body was enchanting. Henry ran a hand slowly up from Jaden's stomach to his collarbone, admiring the view. Emboldened by Jaden going first, Henry was more confident by the time he shifted onto his elbows and pulled his own T-shirt off. He tossed it aside and lay back, his heart pumping with nervous tension all over again.

It was strangely more vulnerable than ever before to bare his skin, like Henry was baring his soul at the same time. No longer was he hiding parts of himself—physically or otherwise. He didn't have layers of disconnect from himself to hide behind, either.

"Sexy," Jaden moaned in appreciation. His gaze lingered briefly on the pale white scars across Henry's chest, but he didn't focus on them. He ran his fingers gently up and over them, into the numb patch around one of Henry's nipples.

Henry blossomed with pride. The compliments validated that small, scared part of him that had never quite gone away. Hearing that Jaden was into this—into *him*? It was exactly what he needed.

"Why, thank you," Henry chuckled deeply. But he felt bad —and a little amused—that Jaden was putting all this effort toward turning him on in a way that wasn't going to work. He had a lot of explaining ahead of him.

So he gently slid his fingers between Jaden's and pulled his hand away from his chest, then gripped his hip and pulled him on top of him.

Jaden made a soft, adorable squeaking sound and beamed, leaning down to press his lips on Henry's. As Henry looped an arm around his back, the smooth warmth of Jaden's chest and the flutter of his heartbeat tantalized him.

Jaden ground against him in a smooth ripple, making heat shoot straight to the tip of Henry's cock. His stomach flipped as pinpricks of heat flushed through him. Unlike his chest, his nerves down south had healed plenty fast, and he was itching for more.

It was impossible to miss Jaden, hard and needy. Those loose silky pajama bottoms didn't stand a chance at hiding it. Fuck, he wanted to be hard, too. *In a minute*, he told himself, squirming under Jaden and deepening the kiss.

Henry sucked Jaden's lower lip, tightening his arms around Jaden's back to pin them together as Jaden ground into him. God, he'd forgotten how fucking erotic it was to feel the effect he was having on another man.

This was more spontaneous than Henry had been in so long—or Jaden, from the sounds of it.

But it felt *right*. Henry was slow to trust in general, but God, he already trusted Jaden. Was that crazy? A mistake? Maybe, but damn it, he was going to commit to it and find out.

Those lips were fierce on his, Jaden finding his confidence and coming into his own. He was guiding Henry, and Henry finally got to let go and enjoy.

And then Jaden's hand wandered to his waistband, and on instinct, Henry tensed up. Years of having to have *that* conversation flickered back to his mind in an instant.

Henry fiercely pushed back against his thoughts. This was different. *He* was different.

"Sorry," Jaden murmured, pausing. He tried to pull his

hand away, but Henry quickly covered his hand and guided it down again.

"No, it's okay. I want you. But my dick works a bit differently. I can explain it."

"Ooh. I get an operating manual?" Jaden teased with a gentle smile.

"Unlike life, yes," Henry giggled, almost breathless with relief. Even though Jaden had been wonderful, he'd half-expected him to react like most guys confronted with anything even a little bit different. Henry didn't want to be left doing all the work with none of the pleasure.

But instead, Jaden leaned down to press his lips on Henry's. "Show me," he whispered, his breath hot against Henry's kiss-swollen lips. "I want to make you feel good. Can I make you come? I really want to, Henry."

Jaden wanted him, and not because of or even in spite of who he was, or what his body looked like, or what he could do for him.

And that swept away the last of Henry's anxieties, leaving space for arousal. It knocked him off his feet and left him breathless, unprepared for the full force of his need.

Henry nodded hard. "More," he whispered. "Touch me."

Jaden slid his hand into Henry's waistband, fingers grazing over the still-numb spot inside his hip. Then he found Henry's shaft and squeezed gently, his eyes widening. "Big boy."

Henry gave him a loopy grin of relief and joy. The prickles of heat that tingled through him were newly intense. He knew what it felt like to touch himself these days... but having another man explore his body? That was new, and deeply erotic.

"Wanna find out how big?" Henry teased.

"I'd love to." Jaden pulled his hand out and knelt back, tugging Henry's PJ pants down. He helped Henry kicked them off and then did the same himself. Then he scrambled for his backpack and pulled out a small tube of lubricant, which made Henry prickle with excitement at what that meant.

When Jaden finally straddled Henry again, both of them naked and glowing with excitement, Henry's eyes fell to that magnificent sight above him. Jaden was hard and flushed pink, his cock curved gently up toward his belly and glistening wet at the tip.

Henry licked his lips, stroking a hand with an overhand grip down his own shaft. He loved the burst of pleasure that ignited deep within his belly, and the way Jaden stared, wide-eyed.

"Don't worry," Henry grinned. "It doesn't get any bigger—just harder." He was definitely a shower, not a grower.

Jaden sheepishly giggled. "Good. I like a big dick, but phew... I wasn't sure you could fit any more inside me. You're going to fill me up, Henry." He kneaded Henry's chest gently, his eyes wide and pleading. "Right?"

Even hearing him talk dirty like this made Henry burn with need. "Oh, I will," he promised Jaden in a low growl, stroking himself again. His cock was velvety, soft around the outside and firmer in the middle. "But first, a quick lesson."

"I'm paying attention, teacher," Jaden batted his eyelashes innocently. "Will there be a test...icle?" He clearly couldn't resist the joke, giggling again.

"Several," Henry said, smirking as he swatted Jaden's thigh. "Now, watch closely."

"I am." Jaden's voice was warm and husky with appreciation and curiosity—a good kind. "Believe me." Jaden's gaze wandered up and down Henry's body, and he sat back on his heels and stroked himself ever so slowly.

Oh, Jesus. Henry could watch Jaden jerk off to the sight of him all day. He stifled his own groan and bit his lip, trying to collect his thoughts. "So, I have pretty good sensation. But I can't get hard on my own. Instead…"

He slid his hand to the base of his shaft and his fingers around to the side, squeezing one of his balls gently. His fingertips instinctively found the trigger under the skin. Air flooded into his shaft, hardening his cock until he was as stiff as the man who kept teasing and grinding against him.

"Ohhh. That's hot," Jaden whispered. "And convenient. I'm kinda jealous. I have to deal with the rises and falls on a whim."

Henry cracked a grin and kissed him. It made his heart sing, hearing Jaden find the advantages to his body instead of focusing on the differences like they were a bad thing. God, he was perfect. "You can pump me up anytime," Henry teased.

"I'll take you up on that, back in Denver." Jaden's voice wavered, even if his words were bold.

Oh my God! Henry nearly vibrated with excitement as Jaden's unspoken question hung in the air between them. It meant so much at once—that Jaden liked him, that he wanted to continue their relationship, and that it wasn't going to be a "let's just be friends" arrangement…

Hope flooded Henry so fast that he lost every other train of thought for a few moments. If he could be lucky enough to make things work with Jaden, he had no doubt it would be worth it. He already felt like they'd known each other for months, not just one day.

Henry nodded fast. "Yes. Yeah, I want to. I didn't think

we'd find this kind of spark so quickly."

"It *has* been a whole day together," Jaden murmured, and then paused. "But… the moment I saw you in the airport, I felt it. Chemistry. You know?"

The chemistry that had drawn Henry to the withdrawn man with a sweet heart hiding out under his fears? Yeah, he'd felt it too. He'd hardly been able to tear his gaze from Jaden all day long. And not just because he was trying to help him through a hard day, but because there was something about him that made Henry want to get to know every single little thing about him, and tell all his friends about the cool guy he'd met, and show him off.

However I can, I'll make sure that it does work out.

"God, yes." Henry grinned. "That chemistry is on fire. So am I right now."

Jaden lit up and winked at him. "Let me help with that." He looked Henry up and down, his hand resting on the scar on Henry's hip. So many scars marked his journey, but Jaden wasn't focused on them right now. Instead, he had an eager smile and light touch as he squeezed lube into his palm. Then he knelt over Henry's lap, gripping both their shafts in one hand and squeezing them together.

"Oh," Henry grunted, heat flooding him. His muscles grew taut with pleasure, his toes curling into the bed as he gritted his teeth.

"Good?" Jaden murmured, but his voice was a light, singsong tease that made it clear he was pretty damn sure it was.

Henry chuckled and nodded slightly. "Understatement." God, it was sexy feeling the tight ring of Jaden's fingers pressing their dicks together.

Jaden let go and squirmed backward on Henry's lap, his

gaze focused on Henry's stiff shaft. He slid a finger along the underside from the base to the tip, his hungry gaze focused on Henry's face. "I want to know what feels best."

"Pretty much the same as any guy," Henry managed. All sensation pooled around one fingertip made him almost oversensitive, twitching with pleasure. "The base feels best."

Jaden slid his hand back to the bottom of the shaft, where the lightest touch made Henry's whole body light up. The slickness of his palm helped skin glide over skin without catching—smooth and perfect.

"Yes," Henry gasped, unable to bite back the moan. "There. Fuck."

Jaden giggled softly. "You're even hotter when I have you in the palm of my hand. So to speak. I'm glad I didn't take the couch."

Henry slid his hands up Jaden's thighs, resting one hand on his hip and sliding the other toward Jaden's cock. He wrapped his hand around the throbbing shaft and squeezed gently.

"Oooh, yes," Jaden moaned. His grip on Henry's cock tightened.

Henry stroked in long, slow motions, trying to match Jaden's pace. It didn't take long before their breathing grew quick and ragged. The rest of the world slipped out of focus as they became the center of their own little world.

Jaden squeezed tightly around the base of Henry's cock, the firm ridges of his fingers enveloping him. Meanwhile Henry kept his grip a little looser around Jaden's firmer skin, his fingers slippery around the sensitive head of his dick.

They quickly found their rhythm, exchanging breathless smiles like they couldn't believe they were so lucky. Fate had smiled on the day of that raffle.

"You feel great," Henry whispered, rubbing his fingers along the ridges and veins of Jaden's more textured shaft. It was silky and firm, and the weight in his hand—the knowledge he was wringing ecstasy from Jaden with every stroke—turned him on like crazy.

"Let me frot again," Jaden whispered, carefully nudging Henry's hand out of the way. He gripped both shafts in one hand. This time he kept his grip lower and tighter, letting the heads of their cocks bump and the shafts slide naturally.

Henry whimpered, his whole body stiffening at the sparks that shot through him. He gave in to the waves of arousal swamping him, just gripping Jaden's hips as tight as he dared.

"Good?" Jaden whispered.

Henry arched off the bed as Jaden stroked both hard cocks together. "Fuck! Yes!"

He was clinging to the edge already. He'd never imagined someone else's hand alone could feel so incredible. There was so much more *subtlety* to his arousal now that he was able to stop and linger in his own skin and thus the moment he found himself in.

Getting to feel his hard cock pressed against another man's hard-on for the first time? It was like nothing else, this raw, masculine passion of bodies and souls colliding at the perfect moment in time.

Every sense was heightened, from the sheets brushing against his bare skin to the tiniest whimpers and gasps that slipped from Jaden's lips as he breathlessly ground against Henry's dick. His hips moved in little jerks as he rode against Henry's cock, and it was all too easy to picture him riding *on* it now.

Henry's muscles were already drawing tight, his eyes

squeezing shut for a second. *Damn it, I can't hold on.* As much as he wanted to, it had been so long since he'd been intimate with anyone. Jaden, naked and whimpering against him as he was, turned him on so fucking fast.

"I'm gonna come in, like, two minutes flat," Henry warned breathlessly.

Jaden laughed. "Good. Because I will too. And unlike you, I can't keep it up afterward."

Henry laughed and pulled Jaden down to kiss him. He poured his appreciation into it—for Jaden's bright eyes and his bravery, his sexy little ass and his compassion.

Jaden made Henry feel like he was on top of the world. He was the whole fucking package. God, it blew Henry's mind to fantasize about all the things they could do together. But just getting to feel this here and now was almost enough.

It was perfect. *Jaden* was perfect.

Jaden's lips were sweet and soft as honey, but this was no time for gentleness. They kissed open-mouthed, gasping for breath, hot and desperate. Henry's nails dug into Jaden's back as he clutched him tight. He finally needed release from this tension even more than he wanted to draw it out.

Jaden's cock throbbed against Henry's, the hard ridge of the head sending a deep, pulsating heat through Henry's body with every stroke of Jaden's hand or thrust of his hips. Every spot their bodies touched burned with pleasure, unbearably sensitive, yet leaving Henry greedy for more.

Then Henry's world narrowed, and his muscles drew taut, and he found himself spilling over the edge. He gasped, nails biting into Jaden's back. "Jaden! Yes!"

"Yes, Henry," Jaden whimpered. "Please, come for me, baby. You're so fucking gorgeous, oh my God."

Henry threw his head back against the pillow, baring his

throat as the orgasm shook him from head to toe. Every muscle rippled involuntarily, his body straining as he clenched deep and tight.

His very fingers and toes tingled, his lips burned from their kisses, and he could hardly catch his breath as his cries faded against Jaden's lips.

"Henry," Jaden groaned. The desperate note in his voice made Henry's eyes fly open. He drank in the sight of those beautiful lips pressed together, his gorgeous light brown eyes wide as his cheeks flushed red and hot. "Henry, I'm gonna come for you. On you. That okay?"

Henry nodded in a quick jerk. "Yes, please. That's so hot," he whispered. "Your turn, baby. Come all over me. Make a mess for us both." He gave Jaden a breathless smile, his gaze drawn down between their bodies as Jaden braced himself on a forearm, half-sitting now.

Henry had almost forgotten how much he loved the feeling of another man's seed splattered across his skin. Since he couldn't ejaculate himself, it was even more special when he got to feel it so soon after his own orgasm—like it was his own, primal and raw and *right*.

Like Jaden was claiming him, and Henry needed him to more than anything in life.

"Yes, I'm so..." Jaden whimpered, letting go of Henry's hard cock. He stroked himself hard and fast, and then his eyes widened as his strokes slowed. Breathless with anticipation, Henry ran his fingertips up Jaden's thighs and around to his ass, trailing one finger around his sexy little hole.

"*Fuck!*" Jaden cried out, clenching hard and throwing back his head. He gasped, his lips silently forming Henry's name as his balls drew tight and he came. Jet after jet of his hot passion spilled like a fountain, splattering across Henry's stomach.

The sight made Henry curl his toes with pleasure, a loopy grin spreading across his face. "Nice load. You can do that anytime."

"Oh, man," Jaden whispered, staring at the sight. He whimpered, clutching the comforter next to Henry's head as he finally let go of himself. "That's... you're... we're hot together." Then he flopped on his side next to Henry, wiping the sweat from his forehead and giggling breathlessly.

"We are," Henry murmured. He kissed Jaden first of all, tender and slow. They were both out of breath and disheveled, but the hazy gleam in Jaden's eyes made Henry smile.

He finally carefully scooted away to grab a tissue. It seemed a shame to clean up so soon, but he had something better: the blissful satisfaction thrumming through his bones.

"Let's do that again. Soon." Jaden eagerly wriggled against the mattress, kissing Henry's shoulder. "Please?"

"Tomorrow morning?" Henry grinned.

Jaden winked. "I was thinking back in Denver. I want to set a date before we leave. I think... I *think* I could be brave enough to leave the house if *this* is what happens."

Henry caught his breath as he threw away the tissue and lay down again, wrapping an arm around Jaden and pulling him close. "Wow. Really?"

"Really," Jaden breathed out. He looked nervous but excited, too. "It's gonna be tough. I know that. But it's worth it. And... um, a relationship would be *really* worth it. With you, I mean."

Bless him, Henry thought, beaming at him. He squeezed Jaden around the shoulders, pulling him into his chest and kissing his hair. He admired Jaden so much for being willing to put himself under that much pressure. "I'll make it easier for you," he promised. "However I can. I want this to continue, too."

It was like Jaden had flipped a switch inside Henry's mind. All his anxieties just melted away in the face of the certainty in his heart.

"Thank you," Jaden murmured with a sleepy little smile. "I'm glad you want more than a one-night stand."

"Oh, I do," Henry assured him, tilting his chin up for one gentle kiss against his lips. "I don't do one-night stands any more than I do single serial-killing." He winked.

Jaden burst out laughing, shoving Henry's chest. "Oh, you. I'd like to serially fuck. And maybe even serially romance. We could serial date."

"Serial date!" Henry laughed. He rolled Jaden onto his back and kissed him over and over until they dissolved in laughter together once more.

Yeah, he wanted to keep this guy around for a long time to come. But would it last beyond this one single, dreamlike moment?

This evening was the perfect bubble for just the two of them, sheltered away from the rest of their lives. There was no denying the obstacles they faced as soon as they woke up tomorrow.

But Henry did know two things for sure: he didn't want to hide himself away from the rest of his life any longer, and he *did* want to help Jaden along his path, too. There was so much more to learn about each other back in the real world.

Could a relationship really come from one night like this?

Tomorrow would tell.

CHAPTER
Nine

JADEN

THE PLANE RIDE BACK TO DENVER FELT HOURS LONGER THAN the outbound trip. Jaden took the window seat, angled his body toward Henry's, and held his hand from takeoff to landing. And bless him, Henry never said a word of complaint. In fact, he spent the flight idly rubbing Jaden's hand.

The plane itself wasn't the hardest part. Even being way up in the sky wasn't the scariest part of it all, because… well, it wasn't *really* outdoors in the sense that Jaden knew. People didn't walk on clouds.

But it was the trudge back through the terminal to the exit that crushed Jaden from all sides.

"Doing okay?" Henry kept a tight hold on Jaden's hand and steered them for the luggage carousel.

"Better than ever." Jaden managed a quick smile over at Henry before he spotted the expanse of the terminal behind him and shivered, looking down at his feet again.

He was glad Henry was taking charge, leading him out of this place, but holding hands also made him more anxious.

They didn't talk about what came next for them until they reached the terminal doors. Then, Henry bit his lip and offered a nervous smile at him. "So, when can I expect the pleasure of seeing you again?"

"You can see me again anytime. Pleasure guaranteed," Jaden teased, glad that it was so easy to flirt with Henry. It was strangely easier to breathe when they weren't holding hands.

Not that strange, his asshole brain reminded him. *Stay alert. Some hateful person might see you... again. It could happen anywhere.*

God, Jaden needed to be home. It pulled him in two as the desire to be with Henry vied with the desire to be *safe*.

Henry beamed at him. "Judging by last night, I'd say so. I have an overnight trip coming up now, but how about I text you when I'm back?"

"Perfect." Jaden took a deep breath to be brave and slipped his fingers between Henry's. "Um... is anyone going to be waiting for you?"

Henry shook his head. "I drove and parked overnight. Did you need a ride back?"

For the first time in his life, Jaden almost wished Spence *wasn't* here for him—but then he felt bad right away. He had no doubt his big brother was here and totally ready to interrogate him.

"No, thanks. My brother's picking me up," Jaden told him with a small smile. "He'll be here already."

"Do you want me to come with you?"

Jaden really didn't want to invite that much teasing from Spence. "No, that's all right."

Henry frowned as Jaden tensed up. "But it won't be long

before we see each other," he said firmly, maybe misinterpreting the reason for Jaden's anxiety.

"Yeah." Jaden let out a shaky breath and smiled. "He'll want to question me, no doubt. I bet Trip will be the same with you."

"Uh oh." Henry pretended to look nervous. "Should I prepare for a hard time?"

Jaden giggled despite himself. "Nah. He's good. He's always trusted me to know my own mind. Whatever I do, he'll support it." And aside from the times Spence drove him out of his mind, Jaden knew he was damn lucky to be able to say that.

"Then I could bend you backward with a goodbye kiss." Henry gave Jaden a wicked grin. "I like a good show."

Jaden snorted at Henry and tugged him by the hand as he walked for the arrivals door. "You're trouble."

"Good thing you like trouble."

"I do." Jaden squeezed Henry's hand, flinching again when someone brushed past.

It was exhausting, being so on-guard all the time, but worth it. The warmth of Henry's hand outweighed the way Jaden's throat burned and palms tingled with fear—not only fear, but fear *of* that fear.

Layers and layers of shit he had to sort through. He had to, with someone like Henry suddenly on the line. Because Henry was still patient and understanding… for now.

Most people had a limited supply of fucks to give, and once those fucks were exhausted, they lost all patience. When his mental illness became inconvenient instead of cute and endearing, people left Jaden like a bat out of hell.

And as understanding as Henry had been yesterday, it

only made Jaden worry more. They were back in the real world. The fall was coming. It had to be, and soon. His agoraphobia, his panic, his tightly-wound fears—it was ugly and frustrating and resentment-inducing even for him, and he was the one with the damn issues.

Medications hadn't helped. Therapy had, but it took time and patience, and he was tired of both.

Thank goodness the awkwardness between them was gone, at least. Whatever happened now, Jaden was pretty sure that Henry wasn't a serial killer.

"You'll text as soon as you're back?" Jaden didn't mean to sound so needy.

"The moment I'm free," Henry promised with an easy smile. He beamed at Jaden, taking his other hand. "So I guess this is goodbye. Thank you for this date. I've never had one like it. I can't wait to see you again."

"You, too," Jaden managed with a dizzy smile. He was so focused on their surroundings that it was impossible to come up with anything better than, "Bye for now."

People parted around them to walk through the arrivals door, but Henry didn't seem to care.

Jaden did. Holding hands while walking close together, where people might not spot the locked fingers, was one thing, but...

No. It's my brain being a dick again. I'm safe with Henry. Safe, remember?

Henry pressed one more kiss on Jaden's lips, and Jaden didn't quite have time to pull himself out of his thoughts to properly return it. But before he could say anything, Henry pulled back, gave a quick wave and bright smile, and he was gone through the doors.

Jaden put one foot in front of the other and focused on that, heading to where Spence had promised to meet him. Time passed, but he wasn't sure how much time.

Until a hearty "There you are, bro!" rang out.

Jaden choked back the relief and followed the sound of Spence's voice into his brother's arms. Spence hugged him tightly, showing mercy by not picking him up off the ground like they were kids again. Nobody seeing their back-slapping hug would mistake it as romantic.

"How'd it go, man?"

Damn it. He had to say something now. His voice cracked the first time he tried, but with Spence by his side—his large frame shielding him from passersby and leading the way—it was easier to give it a second shot. "Gimme a few."

Spence knew not to push when Jaden said this. He just nodded and put a hand on Jaden's shoulder and turned him around to steer him toward the car. The weight was an added reassurance, and by the time they climbed in, Jaden let out a breath of relief and found words.

"It was good. I'm seeing him again."

Spence whooped and pumped his fist. He climbed into the driver's side and grinned smugly across at him. "I knew you could do it."

Jaden tugged the seatbelt as tight as it would go and then gripped it by his hip to pull it even tighter across his lap. Only when he was wedged thoroughly into the seat did he start to breathe deeply and evenly.

"Go me," Spence continued, starting up the car and throwing on the turn signal. "I better be your best man, you know. Or maid of honor. My legs would look great in a dress, and my beard would hold so many flowers—"

Jaden wished he could laugh, but his gut twisted with annoyance. "Wait up."

Spence blinked and looked over at him, taken aback at the interruption. Jaden tended to listen more than talk, especially when he was pulling himself out of a stressful situation. "Huh?"

"You shouldn't have thrown me into that situation in the first place. I wasn't ready."

"But is he the guy of your dreams?" Spence asked with a hopeful smile.

Jaden hated when they argued. He had no choice but to push back. He needed to say this, before it lingered between them. "I don't know. That's not the point. Point is, I wasn't *ready* for it. I panicked several times."

"Did you call your therapist? I mean, she wanted you to go out more, right?"

Jaden worked his jaw around. He didn't want to answer, because the fact that he hadn't would be seen as progress—when to him, it really wasn't. He didn't want to live with Sandra on speed-dial.

As glorious as this past day had been, he'd still gone through the wringer to make it happen. Tired didn't even begin to cover it. Spence meant well, but he didn't understand the toll it took to go through so much in just a couple days.

"No."

"See—"

"No," Jaden snapped. "You're not listening to me. I'm telling you that I wasn't ready. That should be enough. Why do I need a goddamn doctor's note?"

Silence fell in the car, interrupted only by the hum of the

engine and the click of the turn signal as Spence moved lanes.

Jaden recognized his expression—sullen, unwilling to admit he was in the wrong. It took Spence time to get past his feelings about a situation and look at the facts. But Jaden wasn't going to soften the blow, so he bit his tongue and let the silence roll and roll.

Finally, when they were pulling off the freeway, Spence spoke again. "You're snapping at me because you've had a hard couple of days. And I damaged your trust by making you go out to the bar."

"Yeah. That wasn't so bad, only..." Jaden waved around at the outside like they were still at the airport, meaning the whole blind date.

"You weren't supposed to win the blind date." Spence chewed his lip and glanced sideways at Jaden as he waited to turn the corner. "I'm glad you met a great guy, but... yeah, even I wasn't expecting that. I knew you could do it. But I didn't take it seriously, the possibility you'd *win*. I thought it would just be one night and then you could hide out and recover. I'm sorry. I should have listened to you better. Are you all right?"

Jaden knew his brother was doing it because he cared. It still sucked, but it wasn't like he wanted to hurt Jaden. So he drew a breath and let it out. The words sounded like an offer of truce.

"I'll need a couple days to breathe again, but I'm all right," Jaden said.

"By the way, you never said he *wasn't* the guy of your dreams." Spence smirked. "So, what's his name?"

Jaden eyed Spence. They might have come to a truce, but he wasn't quite ready to joke around with his brother yet.

Thank God they were approaching Jaden's apartment building. "Henry."

"Good, strong name. Look at my baby bro, all grown up and dating." Spence reached out to try to ruffle Jaden's hair, and Jaden smacked his hand away.

"Fuck off."

Spence knew perfectly well how Jaden's *last* relationship had ended. But Jaden didn't want to remember it. He'd only end up alone in his apartment thinking about the ugly looks on strangers' faces, and the nights crying alone after a nightmare, clutching a phone while his supposed boyfriend wouldn't pick up, and the quiet Facebook status change back to *single*.

Oh, good. I'm thinking about exactly what I don't want to think about.

But worn out as he was, Jaden lacked the strength to shepherd his thoughts away. *This* was the impact of the last few days—and it was one Spence would never quite understand, because he didn't have to live like this, rationing out his energy.

"We're here," Jaden announced unnecessarily into the silence. "Thanks for the ride." He'd kept his backpack on his lap, so at least he could bail quickly.

"Welcome. See you soon, huh?" Spence offered, his tone careful.

Jaden hated when Spence talked like he was made of glass and Spence wasn't sure what might crack him open.

"Yeah."

Jaden opened the car door and sprinted for the building. Normally Spence might have walked him to the door, but…

They both needed space.

His pocket buzzed, and Jaden hated that he felt compelled

to check it before he'd even gotten to his own door. If only he could slam a door and walk away, he might be a happier person.

But he was the clinger, the needy guy, the one who would check his phone the moment it went off, the one afraid to have a fight and hold the line.

I had such a great time. Can I come over tomorrow, or is that too soon? :)

Jaden blinked a couple times before he realized it was from Henry, not his brother.

Suddenly, he didn't need *quite* as much space to himself. He stepped into the elevator and texted back.

That would be great. Afternoon?

He had a shift at work tomorrow, even if it was from home. It would be a mood-killer to suddenly bust out the laptop and headphones.

Great! See you around 2? I'll need your address too since I didn't plant a tracker on you. Obviously I failed serial killer 101. ;)

Jaden burst out laughing, his chest loosening as he opened his apartment door, walked inside, and leaned on it heavily to close it.

He slid down the door to the ground as the familiarity of his apartment enclosed him like a bubble. He knew every square inch of this apartment, from the spots of carpets that were worn down to the windows that needed washing. As heavy as steel, the feeling of safety sank into his bones and strengthened him. Texting his address took just a few seconds, and then he got a smiley face emoji in reply and a thumbs-up.

Jaden chuckled and pressed his phone to his chest, pulling his knees up and hugging them, pressing his face into his kneecaps.

"Safe and sound," he repeated like a whispered mantra. "I'm safe and sound." Locked away here, he *was* safe from the great big world and everyone who might mean him harm. Safe from trusting too quickly, from letting people in.

But he had a sneaking suspicion that his heart was not on the same page as his logical brain. Not anymore.

CHAPTER
Ten

HENRY

Blue Skies Outfitting was headquartered in a cabin on the edge of Boulder. They attracted a mix of out-of-state tourists and locals curious about the great outdoors on their doorstep. And it wasn't too far from home—one of many reasons Henry had stuck with the company for five years now. He might not make as much as he could running his own outfit, but it came with good health insurance.

And that had enabled him not just to work in his dream job, but to save his own life. He never could have done this job otherwise. Virtually nobody could afford to pay for phalloplasty. The ten grand he'd had to fork out for top surgery seemed cheap by comparison.

Plus their boss, Damien, was cool with Henry being gay. He even advertised to gay groups and sent Henry out with them. But what nobody knew was Henry's medical history. All they knew was that he'd had too many surgeries for a guy his age. They were all relieved that he wouldn't need more time off for a few years.

Henry wished he could be done with surgery forever, but

he'd need an implant replacement when it broke down. The stupid things weren't designed to last more than a decade at the absolute most. But for the time being, the worst was behind him.

It felt incredible that other people saw the person Henry was now, not the one he'd left behind. But his silence was starting to feel more like a too-small shirt. Or a binder. Henry cracked a smile at the thought. He'd been so fucking glad to give the compression garments away after top surgery to a charity that distributed them to trans guys in need.

Henry had explained the wide scars on his chest as a congenital condition and his coworkers had easily accepted it. After all, five years ago, far fewer people had even heard of trans guys. They hadn't asked about the rectangular skin graft scars on his thighs, or the one on his hip that led down into his waistband. All his scars were fading into white now, and Henry hardly noticed them anymore.

Even with today's growing awareness, most people didn't put two and two together unless they were told. After working so hard to be seen as just himself going forward, was it crazy to want to tell people about his past now, too? What did other trans people do?

Henry had no idea. After moving to Denver, he'd never joined any support groups or anything. The only trans friend he'd kept in touch with was Nic, an online friend who'd chosen the same lower surgeon as Henry. He'd been able to talk about his own experiences to help Nic make a decision.

But Henry was starting to realize that he wanted to be open. He didn't want to tiptoe around and pretend he'd been granted the boyhood he should have had; he didn't want Trip to keep questioning why someone as "objectively hot" as Henry was so nervous about dating guys.

He was tired of shaving away little bits of himself to make others comfortable.

"Give it to me now."

Henry stumbled as he locked up the mini-bus and pocketed the keys. "What?"

"The dirt. There's no way you *don't* have dirt. You haven't said a word about your Grand Canyon trip."

Trip leaned on the side of the bus next to him, scratching his short beard. His warm brown eyes were fixed on Henry, not letting him get away. They were just getting ready to take out a crowd of guys on a bachelor party.

God, it was hard to explain why this date had been so significant. It hadn't seemed like Jaden was just experimenting, curious about trying it with a trans guy. And for Henry… feeling confident enough to disclose his past, face-to-face, for the first time in a year? Being treated just as himself in return? Then having the most unbelievably awesome sex of his life? It was like a dream come true.

"Ah, I dunno," Henry said with a shrug and a smile, trying to deflect.

"Did you like him? Did you hate him? Who was it? What was he like?"

This, at least, Henry could say. "He was… amazing. Sweet, kind, gentle. A little bit quiet. Playful sense of humor. Really anxious, but I know how to help with that."

"Is he your type?" Trip grinned. "Did you fuck?" Heat rose in Henry's cheeks, and Trip gasped. "He is! You did!"

Trip knew more about Henry than some of his gay friends. It was hard to admit to them how little sex he had. But he and Trip told each other almost everything—usually much more on Trip's side, given that distinctly lacking sex life.

"Okay, fine," Henry grumbled and elbowed Trip on the way by. "If you're gonna be a nosy bastard, yes, we did."

"Whoa. That's not like you."

Henry bit his lip. There was no way he could explain how *right* it had felt. What a relief-filled high he'd been on, even to contemplate it. And how well it had turned out, coming so hard he just about saw stars—and at another man's hand, rather than his own.

It was the stuff of *years* of fantasies for Henry. But it was too embarrassing to admit that a plain old handjob had left him floating on cloud nine.

"No, it's not. But you only live once, right?" Henry finally met Trip's gaze again and smiled at him. "And we have great chemistry. I'm going to see him as soon as we get back from this trip tomorrow."

"Whoa!" Trip exclaimed. He beamed at Henry. "Look at you. Next up will be your U-Haul moment."

"Oh, shut up." Henry rolled his eyes.

It was a simple party of eight, so two guides would accompany them. They weren't even going very far. Henry hardly had to think about these trips; he knew the landscape and his job so well now.

Henry loved the nights he got to spend outdoors. In some ways, he even preferred it to going out alone, because he loved looking after people so much.

A guide had to know not just the trails, but how to look after his group in every situation. How to light a fire, track animals, collect food from the wilderness in an emergency, first aid, building shelter... a hundred skills that he'd worked hard to pick up over the years. Plus, interpreting everything and teaching it to people who might never have been really outdoors before.

"Great. I'm doing the kayaking group right after we get back. All newbies." Trip pulled a face. "Can't wait to get soaked."

"Oh, boy." Henry laughed. Rescuing people who had flipped their kayaks was inevitably a wet business. "At least it's supposed to be warm."

Trip crossed himself. "Please." He looked around when tires crunched on gravel and then grinned. "I think some of our guys are here."

"Awesome." Henry high-fived Trip. "Let's do this."

It only took one comment before Henry's stomach sank to the floor.

"We're all guys here. No one cares if I take a leak over by the trees, huh?" One of the guests was rising to his feet from his place at the campfire, gesturing toward the trees nearby.

"I dunno. You're not very tree-like, Stumpy," joked another guy. "Do you belong there?"

"Hey! I identify as a tree!" A round of laughter went around the fire in answer as the first guy headed over to the trees, unzipping his pants.

Henry stayed very quiet, focusing on the kettle. He was boiling water on the fire for one last cup of coffee before bed, which he suddenly needed even more than ever.

His hands shook slightly, and he was caught off-guard by how strong the wave of nausea that swept through him was. *It's fine,* he kept telling himself. He was perfectly safe. Even if he spoke up and said something, nobody would guess.

But the moments of terror—walking into his first men's room, getting his first suspicious glare, having men burst in lockless cubicles while he held a hand strategically to make it look like there was something there…

Jesus, bile rose in his throat as the old, familiar clamp of fear tightened around Henry's heart.

He was used to the odd comment catching him off-guard. By now, he'd perfected his neutral face—not visibly taking offense, keeping the hurt out of his face. Just buried deep inside where only he could hurt himself. Not handing them the weapons to twist the knife.

Worst of all, Trip didn't say a word from where he sprawled by the tents, his thumb in a book. Not that Henry would expect him to. It was their job to facilitate a fun trip for their guests, not to educate them.

What would he say? Henry glanced over, but he couldn't read Trip's expression. That anxiety weighed on him far heavier than a couple of guests being idiots. Did he agree, privately? He *was* smiling.

Henry shook his head and took a deep breath. For fuck's sake, he couldn't hang his own fears on one polite smile. But it made him a little less inclined to start that conversation with Trip.

Most tour groups were perfectly fine. It was only the occasional group that caused problems—usually obnoxious straight guys so afraid to touch each other that they constantly made gay jokes. These days, more people thought the same boring "joke" about identifying as some random object was funny. They never knew that the butt of their humor was sitting right there, keeping them safe.

It was a hundred times easier to navigate these situations without fear now that he'd had surgery, at least. Less risk didn't necessarily mean Henry was more confident to speak up, though.

It took all his focus to safely boil the kettle and keep his hands from shaking when he poured the mugs of coffee.

And his hand slipped.

"Shit," Henry hissed, jerking back from the fire and shaking his hand. His own first aid training kicked in instantly, and he grabbed a bottle of cold water to pour over the burn before any of the others had even reacted.

Concern flooded in immediately. "Are you okay?"

"You got an ice pack?"

Henry had to bite back every ounce of sarcasm. *I'd be a lot better if you hadn't said that stupid shit.* He couldn't blame an accident on them, even if it was their fault he'd been so distracted. It was his job not to be distracted, no matter what.

"I'm fine," Henry said shortly instead, but he let one of the guys pass him another bottle of water. He'd have to purify more water in the morning.

He ignored the scorching heat that crawled along the back of his hand as he finished pouring and passing out mugs of coffee.

That had distracted them from their jokes, at least. The energy wound down and everyone headed to bed—the others guys split up, two to a tent, and Trip and Henry in their own pup tents a short distance away.

Thank God, because Henry wouldn't sleep a wink sharing space with anyone who thought those things.

I'm in charge here, Henry reminded himself as he banked the fire so they could safely get to sleep. *I call the shots.*

He waited until everyone else was in their tents. Even if only sheer fabric separated them and he could hear the guys talking amongst themselves, he could take a moment to just breathe and be by himself. Then he idly rubbed his hand before flinching. Frustration coiled like a hot snake in his belly as he grabbed his pack to get out burn ointment.

Once his hand was treated, Henry unrolled the thin, blow-up mattress and the ultra-light sleeping bag in the tent before crawling into it. There was barely enough space to turn around, but he knew how to manage it by now. He wanted his head by the entrance of the tent so he could gaze up at the sky.

And he was rewarded handsomely for it. Although Henry could only see a sliver of the sky from here, with the woods surrounding the clearing, he was breathless at the sight.

As night darkened to deepest black, stars crept out of hiding, twinkling gently through the millions of miles.

And once more, Henry felt small in the best possible way.

What did a couple guys' thoughtless jokes mean in the big scheme of things? *Fuck all, that's what*, he thought. What mattered was him living life the way that made him happy.

And like that, his thoughts were on Jaden.

He accepts me exactly as I am. No stupid jokes. He clearly hadn't known what to say or how to respond, but he'd tried. He'd cared. He'd made Henry come, for crying out loud.

If he told other people, he could help Damien advertise to other groups. Not just gay groups, but trans people and families. They took parents and kids into the wilderness all the time. Maybe some other trans people wanted to know they were safe with someone who understood their needs and wouldn't make them feel like shit out of the blue.

Damien wasn't dumb—and neither was Trip. It was plausible they'd already guessed. They'd seen Henry's scars plenty of times, and trans people were showing up in more TV shows and magazine covers lately.

If they already knew, then what did he have to lose? Henry didn't want to stay locked away in a trap of silence, trading his self-respect for his safety.

He shifted restlessly, watching the thin boughs at the tops of trees blotting out the stars as they rustled in the light wind.

Maybe what Henry wanted was someone to see him and love him just the way he was. And the price was letting people hurt him.

He snuck his phone out of the sleeping bag with enough wiggling and smiled. Signal. That was a rare treat. Kind of like a sign.

He tapped out a message to Jaden. *At the campsite, and the stars are beautiful. Wish I could take a photo for you.*

Almost no sooner had the message sent than he got a reply: *I wish I could see. Can we put that on the bucket list?*

Do we have one of those now? Henry asked, turning onto his side to curl up with his phone. The air mattress wasn't the most comfortable for first-timers, but he'd spent countless nights on it. In a pinch, he could sleep on bare ground.

We could start one :) Though right now it just says "everything" LOL. How was today?

Henry bit his lip, but he decided to share. Jaden had handled everything else just fine. He of all people was aware that not everyone was tolerant. *Great until the end. Guests made some trans bathroom jokes. Brought up a lot of old stuff for me.*

Oh no :(Guess you can't rub bananas all over them?

Henry clapped a hand over his mouth as he tried not to laugh. That made no sense, but it *had* cheered him up. *What??? They aren't paying me enough for that... or cute enough. I'd do it for you though. ;)*

Jaden sent back a crying-with-laughter emoji. *I mean aren't mosquitos attracted to bananas? But TY, I'll make sure I request bananas tomorrow. ;)*

OH! Henry did laugh this time before he stifled it. *No, they use enough Axe to attract the bugs all on their own.*

Ew! Who are they impressing, the bears? Jaden asked.

Henry smiled. Even though his heart and hand still stung, he felt lighter now. *There's a gay joke in there somewhere.*

After a long, exhausting day, he'd expected to be asleep within minutes, but time seemed to shift until it barely registered as he kept texting with Jaden. They went from joking about bears and leather daddies to talking about their days. Before long, they were planning what to cook together when Henry came over.

When Henry's eyes tugged closed irresistibly, he managed to send a goodnight text with a heart. The last thing he remembered that night was beaming to himself when he got a heart in reply.

"How were they?"

It was always the first question Damien asked when Henry got back from a trip to the backcountry.

"Eh," Henry shrugged, tossing the minivan keys on the desk. He'd already unpacked the tents to air out, and dropped the satellite phone off to charge. "Had better, had worse."

Damien nodded. "Doesn't sound great, though."

"Typical guys," was all Henry had to say.

Damien turned in his office chair to face Henry. The little office wasn't much to see, but it served their purposes. None of them spent much time there, all preferring to be outdoors, but admin work got done here. It took up most of the back room of the cabin, and the rest of the space was where they gave introductions to day trips, greeted guests, and debriefed.

"You just say the word and we'll ban 'em from coming back." Damien sounded serious.

Henry waved a hand. "No way, man. It was nothing. They were all right." Still, it warmed his heart that Damien was so quick to jump to his defense. Maybe it *wouldn't* be so bad, after all.

But then Damien probably thought it was a homophobic joke or something. Would he be as quick if he knew it was about trans people? Or would he have laughed along?

Jesus, Henry would be a lot happier without all these thoughts nagging him.

Damien eyed him but let it go. "Great. Oh, so… I saw you don't have anything booked for the next few days. You want a longer trip? I got a gay group, last-minute. Five of them, going out all weekend. I only need one guy. I thought I'd ask you first."

Henry smiled to himself. He loved groups from his own community. And normally he loved spending as much time as possible outdoors. Overnight trips were nice, but rushed. They were so limited in where they could go when they had to be back within a day. But with time, he could wander wherever they might like.

Heading out for days at a time paid well and passed the time. But he'd never had something keeping him at home before. Especially in the last year, Henry had grown used to wandering.

Growing roots was a terrifying and new prospect for him.

"That's sounding like a no," Damien prompted, raising his brows.

Henry cleared his throat and rubbed his neck. "Oh. Sorry, I got distracted. Uh. Sure, I'd like that."

"You sure?" Damien asked. "I think Trip said he'd be up for it too."

"No, I can do it," Henry firmly said. There was no point in avoiding it—Jaden would have to get used to him spending time away from him. Besides, they weren't even officially dating.

Oh, man. He wanted to spend as much time with Jaden as possible. He was crushing *hard*. Maybe Trip was right about that U-Haul.

But could two guys as opposite as Henry and Jaden *really* click now that they were home, with all the cares of the world upon them?

It was time to find out.

CHAPTER
Eleven

JADEN

JADEN SLAMMED THE CUPBOARD SHUT AND THUMPED HIS HEAD against it, bracing his forearms on the countertop. "What am I going to do?"

The last few days had been tough. A phone call with Spence that morning had underscored their difference of opinion instead of bringing them closer again. It was probably Jaden's fault for doubling down on his annoyance instead of giving his brother the benefit of the doubt.

But Spence *had* pushed him too hard into doing this when he wasn't ready. Even if the outcome was perfect, Jaden hadn't asked him to help him change.

It made Jaden feel like maybe Spence was starting to see him as a burden. Could he blame him? After the last few years of looking after Jaden, Spence might want to go and live his own life.

Jaden's groceries were starting to run low. Sure, he had cans of soup and bread—the important stuff—but nothing he could cook with like fresh veggies. He hadn't expected to be cooking to impress anytime soon.

Henry was back from his bush trip today, and on his way over any time now. He was just stopping to shower first. And even though Jaden was so excited to see Henry, this shadow of dread tempered his excitement.

"Ugh, I can't feed him cans of tomato soup," Jaden mumbled. There was no way to make that a romantic afternoon of cooking for two. After texting playfully about what to cook together, Jaden had to face the actual facts of his cupboards.

Jaden knew perfectly well that he was overreacting a little bit. The leftover exhaustion and stress from pushing himself so far outside his comfort zone was like a fog, slowing his thoughts and making him fixate on one point in the distance.

Sandra, Jaden's therapist, had been impressed as hell that he'd made it through the date without any bigger meltdowns. And that had released something in Jaden's chest—a knot of stubborn frustration that he hadn't done *better*.

Goddamn it, he'd taken the leap of a lifetime. He'd done really fucking fantastically, actually.

Phone therapy was his usual—it was easier than leaving the house weekly. Every month or two, he went out for a session in her office, but it was always a big deal when he did.

And he always had this recovery period for a day or two afterward when everything in his life just seemed *hard*. Except, usually, his dick. That had had a mind of its own these last few days.

Jaden blushed at the thought, which brought him full-circle to his current worry again.

I just want to impress him. Jaden bit his lip and slid to the kitchen floor, which was one of his favorite places to sit when he was moping. That and the corner of the living room, where the paint was scuffed from so many afternoons curled in a tight ball. Thankfully, those days were rare now.

Jaden's phone chimed. He groaned and dug it out of his sweatpants pocket. There was no more delaying the inevitable.

Ready to see a friendly face? :) Henry's text read.

Despite himself, Jaden smiled as the butterflies sprang to life in his stomach again.

More than :) Just one thing. Um, I can't find anything good to cook with! Spence hasn't picked up groceries for me yet and I'm kind of running low. Sorry :(Is soup OK?

Jaden bit his lip, embarrassed at himself. If only he could get over himself, grab his car keys, go downstairs, drive to the store, choose the right foods, check out, come home, and unpack them.

Oh, fuck, that sounded like a week's worth of bravery. Jaden had spent everything he had just staying calm in that helicopter, much less the rest of it.

No problem. I'll bring Chinese!

Jaden's shoulders sagged with relief and his stomach rumbled at the very suggestion. Wait, had he forgotten to eat again? He couldn't remember. Without work today, the hours had blurred together. He'd asked for more shifts, but his call center work from home was always unpredictable. He was up at odd hours to take the shifts he could, and he was grateful for them.

That would be amazing! Thank you!

Henry was legitimately perfect. Jaden's heart swelled that much more as he beamed to himself.

My pleasure. Can't wait to see you.

You too!

Jaden tossed his phone on the floor and covered his eyes

with his hands, allowing himself a little squeak. Then he hugged himself, shivering and squirm-dancing with nervous excitement.

Suddenly it felt like a real date, even though Henry was coming over to see him at home. So Jaden rushed to get showered and changed, his stomach flipping with anticipation.

It was going to be so strange, having someone else in his space. And not just anyone.

For once, it was a real life guy who wasn't Spence. Not a coworker seeing a tiny sliver of the wall behind him while on a training conference call, not his brother coming over with groceries, not the delivery driver dropping off essentials.

A man was romantically interested in Jaden, and he was spoiling him with attention and care. It made all Jaden's half-formed fears of being *too weird for anyone to date* slip away.

It wasn't like his safe bubble was being punctured. Quite the contrary, Jaden was excited to welcome Henry into it—into his real life. They'd gotten along so well that it felt like Jaden's whole life had shifted in just a few days.

Jaden could be himself: at ease, in his comfort zone, without his anxiety making everything feel bright and loud and too much. That really had been one hell of a first date. And now he had no idea what to expect from the second.

Strangely enough, he liked it that way.

When Henry showed up, he was laden with bags. At least two in each hand. Had he bought enough Chinese to feed the whole neighborhood?

"Jesus!" Jaden exclaimed as he pulled open the door. "I mean, uh—hi."

Henry laughed and stepped inside, then leaned in and puckered up, as if waiting for a kiss. It was actually adorable. Especially the way his nose scrunched as he did it.

Jaden giggled and pecked Henry's lips, suddenly dizzy with joy at seeing him again. With Henry right here on his doorstep, their blind date didn't seem like a dream anymore.

"Hi yourself," Henry answered, his voice a low, smooth shiver straight to Jaden's toes. Then he straightened up and smiled, hefting the bags. "I have Chinese. And I bought groceries on the way, too. Hope you don't mind."

Oh, God. Jaden's cheeks burned with surprise as he opened his mouth and failed to come up with words. When he did, he squeaked and cleared his throat. "Um—no. I mean, thank you. That's really... super sweet of you."

Henry chuckled softly. "It's my pleasure." The distinctive smell of fried rice made Jaden's stomach grumble again. He blushed, but Henry just laughed. "Shall we eat?"

"Let's," Jaden agreed. He beamed and led Henry to the kitchen to grab plates and utensils.

He took the grocery bags from him and then hesitated, spotting the red mark on Henry's hand. "Are you okay?"

"Oh, that? I'm fine," Henry said with a laugh and kissed Jaden's cheek. "Thanks. I'll get these to the table."

Watching Henry covertly check out the place made Jaden see it with fresh eyes—as much as he could when he knew every inch of the apartment better than anywhere else.

It was cozy, but the view was gorgeous. Green parkland rolled into hills and then the mountains that always hovered on the edge of the Denver consciousness. It more than made up for the cramped living room space.

Jaden dipped into the kitchen, which was tucked away in an alcove off the living room, to put away groceries. He found himself smiling at Henry's choices. He'd filled one bag with fresh veggies and a bottle of juice, and another with milk, butter, cheese, and pasta. The third had eggs, bacon, and chicken breasts.

Oh, man. There was easily enough for a week, but Henry hadn't broken the bank on gourmet groceries, either. It told Jaden so much about Henry: he was sensible and frugal, exactly the sort of practical man he wanted in his life.

Okay, stop mooning over cheddar cheese and get the damn plates, Jaden told himself, grinning and shaking his head.

When he got to the table and set down the plates and utensils, Henry already had the cartons arranged and open in the middle of the table. He dropped into his seat and grinned as Jaden sat, too. "Come on, dish up what you want."

"But what I want isn't on the menu." Jaden's eyes sparkled as he beamed over the table at Henry, his heart already flip-flopping with the tension in the room between them.

One sweet kiss was nice. But he wanted a lot more. The last few nights, he'd missed Henry's company—to a ridiculous degree, considering they'd only ever spent that one night together.

Henry grinned back at him and held his gaze. "I haven't shown you the dessert menu."

Jaden almost whimpered, clutching his plate against his chest for a moment before he managed to breathe. *Eat first,* he reminded himself. They had time to explore each other's bodies again later—one type of hunger at a time.

Thankfully, as Henry described his camping expedition and Jaden talked about his therapy and shifts at work, the conversation grew less innuendo-filled. They could actually focus on each other, learning as they listened.

It felt adorably domestic. Jaden could almost imagine a future where this was the everyday. Henry getting home from a trip and bringing takeout to celebrate, talking about their days over the table, Jaden pulling him to the couch to watch a movie and cuddle…

Oh, God. It hurt, how much he wanted it. Jaden had never felt the instinct to be with anyone else so strongly before—to *nest* with them, and make a home and a life together.

Was it totally bizarre to think that this was the one?

Jaden lost track of what Henry was saying for a few moments as desire and confusion swelled in his chest at the same time.

"Huh? Sorry," Jaden mumbled when he realized Henry was looking at him.

"It's okay," Henry said with a quiet laugh. "I was just asking what kinds of takeout you like."

"Pretty much anything. I get it a little too much," Jaden admitted, blushing. "Sometimes I don't have the energy to cook or go out and grab something."

It was hard to admit. The little voice in the back of his head that whispered that Henry would soon figure out that Jaden was just one step removed from the guy living in his parents' basement playing computer games all day.

But as always, Henry didn't seem to judge. He just nodded slowly. "Is getting groceries a problem? I could go shopping for you more often. I'm only twenty minutes away. It wouldn't be a big deal," Henry offered, his voice cautious but determined, like he wanted to help but he wasn't sure if he was going to offend Jaden.

Jaden smiled at him and reached over the table to touch

his hand. "Thank you. But... having you shop for me instead of Spence isn't really any better for me, you know? I love that you want to help, but I don't want to grow dependent on you."

"I hear you," Henry said. He bit his lip for a moment before he pushed back. "But aren't we all interdependent?"

"Yeah." Jaden picked up his chopsticks again, nudging his toe gently against Henry's foot. He liked being in contact, even a little bit. "It's for my own sake that I want to get better. I'm tired of this life of hiding and fear. Sandra—my therapist—wants me to have more positive experiences."

"Is that going to help? Pushing yourself more? I don't know much about agoraphobia specifically," Henry admitted. "I just don't want you hurting yourself by trying too much too fast."

"I know what I'm capable of," Jaden reassured him, his stomach rolling as he spotted it for the first time. Henry was sweeping in to rescue him—just like Spence had. Jaden couldn't let that become a pattern, or their fears for him hold him back.

It was hard to explain how the pain and discomfort of staying in his home outweighed the pain of challenging his fears. But at the same time, nobody else could push him into that confrontation. That would only make things worse.

"See, I have to go out sometimes and try things that scare me. That helps me give myself evidence that I'm okay." Jaden smiled. "I started off scared of holding hands in public, and then of being by myself in public, and then just anywhere too big and outside of my safe zone. I grew so afraid of being afraid that..." He gestured around, his chest unexpectedly tight as he set down his chopsticks. "This is where I've ended up."

Henry swallowed hard and nodded. "I see," he murmured. His hand rested on the table halfway between them, like he wanted to take Jaden's. "Thank you for telling me that. I think I get it now—a little bit, anyway. Was our blind date more helpful than harmful?"

Jaden gave him a wobbly little smile. "Very much so. Having you by my side..." he trailed off.

How could he explain it? It wasn't like a wonder drug. He'd still been nervous. But Henry had been a calm, steadying presence, and his initial worries about being spotted being *too gay* in public with Henry had just melted away.

Not just because he was a big, strong-looking guy that people wouldn't mess with—the total opposite of Jaden. But his very energy was so chilled-out that it made it hard to feed back into a cycle of anxiety.

"Tolerable, I hope," Henry winked.

Jaden laughed softly. He had no idea. "You could say that."

After lunch, Jaden left the dishes for later and headed for the couch, patting the spot by his side. "This is my favorite view," he said with a smile.

"Oooh." Henry sat, putting an arm around Jaden as smooth as butter. The early afternoon light against the peaks threw them into a soft, peaceful relief. "Me, too. I love the outdoors. More from within than without."

Jaden nodded slightly. "You're a country guy and not a city boy?"

Henry made a face, which made Jaden laugh. "I don't like the city at all. It always makes me feel... barren." He searched for words. "Hungry for something else? Definitely irritable. Being inside for too long is like breathing through a pillow."

"Right," Jaden murmured, wistfully eyeing the mountains again.

What he wouldn't give to be outside, reveling in the open air. Sure, his apartment was tidy and well set-up—it had to be, since he spent his life here. The first couple of years of messy surroundings had taken a toll on his mental health. But even if it had been made of gold, his home was a cage right now. Jaden didn't want to live his whole life like that.

"Have you always wanted to be a guide, then?" Jaden asked to distract himself.

"Yeah, always," Henry said with a smile. "I hated playing inside. Even when it rained, I was in the yard splashing around in puddles. I'd hate to be trapped..." Henry trailed off, then shot Jaden a guilty look. "Sorry. I don't want to make you feel like shit."

Jaden laughed softly. "It's okay. I do that to myself enough." It was less self-deprecating than it sounded to an outside ear, more of a gentle poke at himself.

Henry squeezed Jaden around the shoulders. "If you ever want to get outside... well, you know I'm down for it."

"Could we?" Jaden gave him a tentative smile, then looked at the mountains. "Could we try, soon? Maybe in a week or two, whenever you're free?"

Henry lit up. "I'd love to. And in the meantime, I'll visit you however much I can." Then he stumbled over his tongue and stuttered. "I-I mean, uh, however much you want me here."

Jaden chuckled gently, nuzzling Henry's shoulder. It was good to hear him so flustered. He didn't feel quite so dumb for his own puppy love. And he loved the chance to cuddle. It was strangely comfortable to be physical with Henry. Sure, it made sense—they'd already had sex, after all—but not fully.

Jaden couldn't explain the way that holding Henry made him need him more, not less.

Like every time he brushed the stove, he burned a little hotter.

"As much as you can," he assured Henry. "If you don't get bored of this place."

"No, I like it," Henry said quickly. "It's small. Cute. Good for one person. I rattle around my house when I'm at home. Feels lonely sometimes."

There was a lot hidden in those words. Jaden rubbed Henry's chest gently and waited to see if there was more.

"My parents are cool, but they have their own life back home in Aurora." Henry smiled a little to himself. "So it's mostly me keeping myself company. How about you?"

"Well, you know about my brother." Jaden made a face. "When we're getting along, that is."

"Ah," Henry murmured with a sympathetic smile. "Is it still about him pushing you into the date?" His voice was gentle and neutral, making Jaden feel like he could tell him anything.

"Pretty much. Hey, you'd make a good therapist," Jaden teased. "He wants me to push myself, but... I was already getting ready. I'm about to get an emotional support dog and everything. And then he took the choice out of my hands and threw me in the deep end. Consent isn't just about sex," he said with a chuckle.

"Ah," Henry breathed out. "Sorry. That's rough, especially when it's your brother."

"It kinda is," Jaden admitted. "But at the same time, I met you, and I wouldn't trade that for the world."

Were those words too strong for how little time they'd known each other?

But Henry had offered him the chance to change and grow with his full support, along with love and sex and friendship and acceptance. Everything Jaden had been missing. Maybe that was why holding him made his chest ache with the realization that he'd been missing it all for so long.

Henry just murmured, "Me, neither." His smile was gentle and warm.

And it stoked the determined fire inside Jaden—the one that said the time was right to do this. To change his life. To take a breath, and be brave, and step into the big unknown.

Lots of people got attacked for being gay. Or for other things, like the color of their skin, or the clothes they wore, or taking up two parking spaces instead of one. And lots of people survived it, too. Jaden was tired of crumbling. He wanted to rebuild—this time, on a solid foundation.

Jaden tried to shrug off the thoughts racing through his head and instead looked up at Henry. He wasn't even sure what he was asking for. Distraction? Sympathy? Help? Rescue?

But nobody could rescue him except himself.

Jaden's eyes were wet now. Damn it, he hadn't planned to cry on Henry's shoulder. Today was supposed to be a *good* day—a day where he showed Henry how much better he could be than the version of himself that Henry had already seen too much of.

But Henry just slid his arm around Jaden's shoulder and yanked him against his side. And Jaden pressed his face into Henry's shoulder as he curled into him. "I'm sorry," Jaden mumbled.

"No," Henry murmured. "You've gone through a shit-ton in the last few days."

Jaden shook his head. "No, I owe you already."

Henry caught his breath. "No way. Relationships are about give-and-take. Not counting up whose turn it is to cry today."

"Why are you so nice to me?" Jaden mumbled, pulling back and wiping his eyes as he cleared his throat.

Henry just offered him a soft smile. "You deserve to be treated nicely. And you deserve the world. I know what it's like to doubt that, and nobody should feel that way."

Jaden nodded slowly. Henry sounded so fucking wise, he could be a cartoon owl. Was he that much older? He didn't look it. In any case, Jaden felt immature in comparison. "I just didn't expect you to come over, bring food, help me out… it all seems like a lot when we hardly know each other." Which just made him realize something Henry had said: *relationships*. "So, um… are we…?"

Henry cleared his throat, rubbing circles with his thumb on Jaden's shoulder. "I was wondering that myself. We obviously get along."

"Yeah," Jaden laughed. That was an understatement. He still wasn't sure what he offered Henry, but he was trying to keep an open mind and remember all the good things about himself that he'd let go over the last few years.

"And there's no pressure to date or anything if that's not what you want. If you need a friend, I can be that," Henry told him.

Jaden shook his head. "What do you *want*, though?" He didn't want Henry to assume Jaden's needs and work around that, like everyone seemed to do.

Henry hesitated for a few long moments. One of those rare glimpses of uncertainty crossed his face as his gaze flickered between Jaden's eyes. "I want to try dating you."

Jaden giggled with delight, squeezing Henry so hard it hurt. "I'd like that."

Henry's beautiful blue eyes lit up. "You would?"

"Yeah. I really would," Jaden breathed out, suddenly so happy it was hard to speak. "I'm actually looking forward to getting outside with you again. Last time... went well, despite everything. But maybe not the biggest, scariest place in the whole US."

"We can give that a miss," Henry agreed with a laugh that filled the little living room.

"And maybe I can hold hands with you in public." Jaden's palms went damp just thinking about it. "Get past the fears about that, too. I'm ready to get through this, I know I am. I'll just be a mess while I do."

"Change *is* messy. I admire the hell out of you for being brave enough to do it anyway," Henry told him softly.

Jaden laughed and shook his head. "It's not brave. Not like you've been, going through everything you've gone through to be yourself. It's just what I need to do."

"Can we meet in the middle?" Henry countered. "I don't like to think of myself as brave any more than you do. I just... did what I had to do, too. That's not because I *wanted* to be brave. I just had to."

Jaden nodded hard. "Yeah. I don't want to go through all this. But I don't have a choice, and I can either keep holding myself back or..."

"Or take the leap," Henry finished, his voice soft and full of that wonderful compassion and understanding he seemed to bring to every conversation with Jaden.

For once, Jaden didn't feel like a freak talking about his life or future. He didn't have to pretend to be better than he was. Henry had already seen him at his worst, and for some reason, he'd liked what he saw.

So maybe he could love Jaden at his best.

Jaden looked up at Henry, noticing his lips so soft and close. He leaned in to press one long kiss against Henry's lips. For the first time in years, he felt sure of himself.

"I want to leap."

CHAPTER

Twelve

HENRY

It seemed like a dream when Henry finally stirred into wakefulness. He recognized Jaden's smell instantly, the flutter of hair by his nose, the feeling of his warm skin pressed firmly against Henry's front.

Last night they'd made out, tenderly, for a long time. They'd talked for hours on end—until dawn cracked the long, sleepy darkness. Even then, the bubble hadn't shattered. They'd curled up together in Jaden's bed, scarcely able to sleep, stirring every few hours to smile and nuzzle into each other.

Even now, as morning drew into afternoon and the sunbeams crept across Jaden's bedroom floor, Henry's heart fluttered with sharp pangs of excitement. This thing between them, so tender and new—he wanted to shelter it against the winds of life.

Jaden stirred, pressing back against Henry's body. A surge of desire coursed through Henry at every inch of smooth skin sliding along his own. He caught his breath, enjoying the pinpricks of heat that danced down to his belly and beyond.

I haven't had good morning sex in forever, Henry thought, smiling to himself. For years, he'd found it easiest to fuck in the darkness when he could sleep to escape the exhausting whirl of thoughts that struck afterward.

Now, though… it was a delicious mental image.

Henry's arm was draped around Jaden's waist, his hand flattened against his chest. He rubbed in a slow circle and then brushed his fingertips across one of Jaden's perfect, pointed nipples.

"Nnnh." Jaden's long, low sound was soft but pleased, half-awake.

The sound made Henry's dick throb instantly, his mind taking him right back to the last time he'd seen Jaden come— all over him.

He swallowed hard, almost quivering with impatience as he let his fingertips glide in little circles around and over Jaden's nipple. He knew it was a hot button for most guys, though some were more sensitive than others.

Jaden was *very* sensitive. He whimpered and then stretched and squirmed against Henry. That sexy little ass pressed into Henry's thick, throbbing, soft length. It made Henry's stomach flip with the fire that was suddenly burning away every lingering moment of laziness.

"S'good," Jaden mumbled into the pillow, his face still turned downward and one arm flung over his head.

Henry grinned to himself and pressed his lips to the back of Jaden's neck, pinching his nipple and rolling it slowly between his fingers.

It was impossible to miss the sharp gasp and the way

Jaden stiffened. With their legs tangled, Henry even felt the tremble that passed through Jaden's thighs.

Jaden pressed back into Henry so hard he could feel the ridges of his spine pressing into his breastbone. His fingers curled into the pillow, gripping it tightly as his breathing grew shallow and quick.

"Good morning, sweetheart," Henry murmured. He walked his fingers up to the other nipple and flicked the very tips of his fingers quickly across it.

"Fuuuck," Jaden groaned, almost inaudibly from under the pillow and the crook of his arm.

A soft laugh burst from Henry. "What was that?" He scraped his nail in a slow circle around the sensitive nub, curious just how sensitive he was—and how far he could push Jaden.

"Good fucking morning to you, too," Jaden mumbled, his voice rough and low. He shifted, bringing one hand down and under the sheets.

Henry couldn't see what he was doing, but he could certainly feel the shift of the bed and the way he clenched and gasped all of a sudden.

Jaden shifted, not quite lying on his back, resting against Henry's chest and kicking one leg across Henry's legs. The sheets settled over his lower body, and they rose and fell with his hand.

That was a *much* better view.

Henry grinned to himself and mouthed at Jaden's neck. "Got a little morning wood problem there?"

"I wouldn't call it a problem." Jaden twisted, straining around until Henry could peck his lips. "More of an opportunity."

Henry laughed again, his whole chest glowing with affection. Jaden was adorable. "I agree." He ran his hand slowly down Jaden's belly, admiring the soft trail of hair that led down from his belly button. It widened into a coarse patch, and then the tips of his fingers brushed against the base of Jaden's shaft.

"Yes," Jaden hissed, his hand giving up its slow, firm pace. Instead he covered Henry's fingers, guiding his hand up to close around his swollen shaft.

"God, that's hot," Henry moaned. He kissed a trail along Jaden's neck to his shoulder, then bit lightly as he squeezed and started stroking.

Jaden whimpered and ground back against Henry. "I want to get you hard, too."

"You might need a tutorial." Henry grinned to himself as Jaden turned onto his back now and groped up his thigh.

"That's okay. I want to learn." Jaden pressed his cheek into Henry's shoulder and gazed up at him with those big, dark eyes. "I definitely won't use this power for evil."

Henry threw back his head and laughed. "Oh? What are you planning?"

"Noooothing," Jaden chirped in a sing-song voice, blinking innocently. His fingers slid across Henry's thick shaft, making Henry flinch and gasp with pleasure.

"Whatever you're up to, watch out," Henry warned Jaden, grinning. "Two can play at that game. And I can get you hard without even touching you."

"You've done that plenty this week," Jaden murmured, making Henry shiver with pleasure. "You're already turned on, though, right?" Jaden murmured as he wrapped his hand around Henry.

"Fuck, yes," Henry told him with a quiet laugh. He bit his lip at how incredible the tight ring of Jaden's fingers felt.

With every stroke, Henry's skin slid across the rigid core of his cock.

Jaden's fingertips glided over Henry's balls, and then he hesitated. Henry pulled his hand away from Jaden's cock and rested it on Jaden's, guiding his fingers to the side where he knew the trigger lay. "Squeeze," he murmured.

"It goes against every instinct to squeeze you *there*," Jaden murmured back with a laugh. But he gingerly did so, and then sucked in a quiet breath. "Oh, I *see*."

Henry's shaft started to harden, and Jaden squirmed with delight. "Oh!"

"A couple times," Henry encouraged him, grinning. It *was* delicate, but the pump was also firm, designed to hold up to years of manhandling.

"There," Henry murmured and let go of Jaden's hand to take hold of his cock again instead. "And now you know."

"That is so cool," Jaden breathed in awe. "When you get over the hill, you won't have to worry."

Henry chuckled, pressing his lips against Jaden's jaw. "And I can come without ever getting hard. Or making a mess."

Jaden gave an envious moan that made Henry's chest swell—and his cock twitch involuntarily as he clenched down with a pleasurable twinge. "Bet that makes middle-of-the-night jerks so much easier," Jaden murmured. "Does everything feel good the way I'd expect? You like it here the most?" He slid his hand to the base of the shaft and squeezed.

"Fuck," Henry grunted, his muscles going taut as sensation exploded inside. It almost hurt, how sensitive he was, but it was fascinating. Something was different now from when he was on his own. Just having another man's touch on him heightened every moment. "Yes," he added with a breathless laugh.

Jaden grinned, and then he squirmed further down the bed. Before Henry knew it, he was crouching between his legs, the sheets up to his shoulders. "I want to taste you," Jaden breathed, his voice dripping with hunger.

Henry gasped, pushing his hands through Jaden's hair and gripping tightly. "Yes. No condom? I don't have any with me. Is that fine?"

Damn it. He doubted he'd fit the standard size Jaden had, and he hadn't remembered to grab them from his overnight bag after their last trip.

But Jaden just grinned, cupping his hand under Henry's balls as he breathed across the tip, "Hell, yeah, that's fine. I'm definitely negative. Or else it's an immaculate infection."

Henry almost wheezed with laughter. "Me, too. Oh my God, Jaden."

But Jaden gave him a mischievous grin, then ran his tongue along the shaft, from base to tip. The flush of heat and wetness that coursed through Henry's nerves made him shiver and gasp. Jaden eagerly wrapped his lips around the head of his shaft, sliding it into his mouth.

Watching himself disappearing into Jaden's gorgeous little mouth made Henry shiver. He tightened his grip on Jaden's hair until the other man whimpered, then gasped. "Sorry."

"Mmm-mmfh." Jaden made it clear without words that Henry was welcome to manhandle him, his cheeks flushing as he grabbed Henry's hand and kept it there for a moment.

Noted, Henry thought, grinning at Jaden.

Jaden's other hand caressed Henry's balls, gently tracing along half-forgotten nerves. His sensation was patchier there, but even that flicker of unpredictable erotic touch drove Henry wild.

"Fuck, that's good already," Henry breathed out. He let go of Jaden's hair but squeezed his shoulders, rubbing his thumbs into his muscles before scratching his back. "*You're good.*"

Jaden wrapped his hand around the base of Henry's shaft and squeezed hard, then started bobbing his head. He choked on the length and whimpered, greedily pushing his mouth down to meet the ring of his fingers.

Every wet noise and flicker of Jaden's tongue against sensitive skin prickled deep inside Henry's shaft, and further into his belly. Alight with desire, he bucked off the bed, thrusting up into Jaden's mouth.

"Fuck, sorry," Henry gasped, trying his hardest to lie still. It was so much more arousing than he'd expected, though! The joy rippling through him, body and soul, was hard to contain.

Jaden held still, his eyes wide and pleading—like he wanted Henry to take over.

So he did, thrusting up into that hot, wet mouth lazily at first. He quickly found his rhythm, flexing in short, sharp movements. When he was sure Jaden could handle it, Henry pushed deeper, until his cock brushed the back of his throat.

He filled Jaden's mouth and then some, but Jaden had it covered. He kept his hand on the base of Henry's cock, twisting gently with each upward thrust.

And fuck, if that didn't drive Henry out of his mind.

His body was tight now, throbbing with unbearable need. However hard he tried, he wasn't going to be able to last. This was like nothing he'd experienced, and he was addicted.

Never before had this hard cock been in another man's

mouth—let alone one as gorgeous as Jaden, who was braced above him on one forearm, whimpering softly as Henry fucked his mouth.

God, he was going to make Jaden come so hard and all over him. That thought alone sent a fresh wave of arousal through Henry, almost enough to spill him over the edge.

"Yes!" Henry grunted as he dug his fingernails into Jaden's scalp. This time there was no stopping—and no way he wanted to. His breathing was ragged, his cheeks flushed. All that mattered was the staccato of his heartbeat, and the swelling surge of *need* pulsing deep within.

Jaden whimpered, the vibrations coursing through Henry as he drew tight deep inside, curling his toes into the bed. Jaden's flushed cheeks and quiet moans were insanely addictive.

"I'm gonna come, baby," Henry gasped, pushing himself up on an elbow to be sure Jaden heard—and because he couldn't tear his eyes away from the sexiest sight of his life.

His own cock plunging deep between those pink lips, the heat and suction against him, the wet surface of Jaden's tongue—and best of all, the tight grip squeezing the throbbing, most sensitive part of his hard cock…

"I can't stop. I need—Jaden, I—oh! Fuck!"

White-hot pleasure burned through him, a wildfire of unbearable ecstasy. Henry collapsed against the bed as his muscles went taut until he almost couldn't breathe—definitely couldn't see, or think.

But he could definitely feel. Oh, every brush of Jaden's shoulder against his thigh, the whisper-soft touch of his hair against Henry's belly, but most of all, the tight purse of his lips around Henry's shaft. Gradually Jaden let the suction go and drew his mouth off Henry, still squeezing him gently until Henry was too sensitive and pushed his hand away.

"That good?" Jaden giggled, wiping his hand across the back of his mouth.

"Jesus," was all Henry could mumble. He was only now aware that he was sweaty and out of breath and vibrating with happiness at a frequency he was sure was physically apparent. "Come here."

When Jaden scooted up the bed, Henry grabbed his hips and kept on pulling him up until he sat on his chest. Jaden squeaked but grabbed the headboard, staring down at Henry with wide eyes, red cheeks, and swollen lips.

"Your turn," Henry growled. "I want to taste you, Jaden. And make you come. Enough for both of us—all over my face. Can you do that for me?"

Jaden's cock twitched in midair, rising toward his belly. He raised his hands to cover his face for a moment, crimson bursting across his nose and even up to the tips of his ears. "Yes," he breathed out raggedly. "Oh, my God. That's so hot, I can't even..." he trailed off in a whimper, trembling above Henry.

Henry smirked. He ran his hands gently up Jaden's thighs to squeeze his ass, making a show of licking his lips since Jaden was peeking through his fingers. Then he leaned in, catching the tip of that gorgeous cock in his mouth.

Jaden's musk was salty-sweet and thick on the tongue. The slit was already wet, and as Henry circled his tongue around the head, it slid smoothly over his lips. Then he kept going, pushing his mouth down the shaft until he took it all in.

All he could taste was Jaden, velvety-soft and heavy in his mouth.

But still, even as he grabbed Jaden's ass and yanked him gently, it took encouragement before Jaden started to move. His thrusts were shallow, uncertain. A long minute passed before he had the knack, and he braced himself on the headboard again.

That's it, my gorgeous, Henry thought. God, he was pleased enough to grin up at Jaden—but his caution prevailed and teeth stayed firmly sheltered under his lips.

"Oh, fuck. Henry, that's good," Jaden gasped, as if surprised. His body gleamed with a sheen of sweat, his breathing ragged as he thrust. His endurance wasn't all there, but no matter—Henry's was.

Henry gripped his hips, squeezing his lips tightly around the flushed shaft. His tongue danced around, prompting whimpers and moans from Jaden, as he bobbed his head in shallow but effective movements.

"Fuck," Jaden gasped, his thighs trembling as he rested his forehead on the wall. "Henry. I can't…"

Good, Henry thought, digging his nails in and moaning long and low. *Don't hold back, baby. Give me all you've got.*

Jaden went taut under his hands, his movements slowing into desperate twitches, and then he threw his head back with a full-throated cry.

God, he was *beautiful,* his body arcing above Henry like a bow drawn tight. His cock swelled in Henry's mouth, and then a jet of his wet, sticky mess hit the back of Henry's throat.

He swallowed hastily, several times, while Jaden pulled back and stroked himself lightly, swaying over Henry. Henry kept his grip tight to make sure Jaden didn't collapse.

The last few spurts landed across Henry's cheek and

mouth, dripping from his chin. He could feel the wet, thick heat of it—and see Jaden's jaw drop.

"Oh, my God. Is that okay?"

"More than okay," Henry murmured. He licked his lips and made a show of swallowing. The musky tang was pleasantly sweet—perfect for a mid-morning dessert.

Jaden whimpered and scooted back against Henry. This time, Henry chuckled and let Jaden collapse flat against him, his weight hardly registering. The slick heat of their bodies sure did, though. He could lie like this all day.

Henry locked his arms around Jaden's back and nuzzled his cheek, kissing his neck and shoulder. "Beautiful," Henry breathed out.

Jaden made a happy little noise. "That was so good. It was good, right?"

"It was *great*," Henry assured him, laughing to himself with a shake of his head. How could he explain?

"Yeah?" Jaden pressed his cheek against Henry's chest as he hugged into him.

"So good," Henry murmured. "First time getting a blowjob since I've been able to get hard on my own. First time without a condom, either. And my sensation has gotten way better. That was... I didn't even know orgasms could wreck me like this." He was bonelessly limp almost all over, yet exhilarated.

Jaden squirmed against Henry's still-hard cock with a giggle. "Good."

Henry chuckled and wrested Jaden to one side so he could reach between his legs and go soft. "There," he breathed out, embracing him again. "Perfect."

It was so gentle and intimate, yet Henry felt so damn

alive. He couldn't lie still, and it didn't take long for Jaden to notice his squirming.

"Restless?" Jaden asked with a mischievous smile.

Henry nodded with a sheepish smile. The glimpse of blue sky outside, the knowledge the day was slipping away... it was hard to just do *nothing* indoors, even if doing anything—including nothing—with Jaden was so perfectly right.

If only we could go out together... But no. He couldn't hold that against Jaden. He knew what he was signing up for.

But Jaden seemed to read his mind. He smiled slightly, stroking Henry's hair. "I was thinking... I might be up for a hike by this weekend. I don't have any shifts yet either of those days."

"Ah, shit," Henry murmured with an apologetic frown. "I have a group booked already."

Jaden hummed, that steely look coming into his eye.

Uh oh, Henry thought. Sure enough, Jaden gave him a firm nod.

"Okay then, today."

Henry caught his breath. "Are you sure? Like, right now?"

Jaden chuckled. The sound was forced, but the determination in his eyes stayed. "I don't want to spend days over-thinking it. Acting like it's a great big deal, when the point is that I want it *not* to be."

Henry followed the logic, and nodded slightly. He didn't want to coddle Jaden, but... he did want to wrap Jaden up in cotton and never let any of his anxious thoughts in again.

But he still had to ask.

"You're not feeling like you have to show signs of progress just for me, are you?"

Jaden blinked at him, and then smiled. "No. No, I want to do this for me. Remember what I said yesterday?"

"I do," Henry confirmed, stroking Jaden's hair gently as he kissed his cheek. Jaden had been so determined that he *was* ready to do this—on his own pace. "Okay, then. Something short? Like a half-hour loop from the trailhead?"

"Perfect," Jaden breathed out. He pushed himself upright, still wobbly, and giggled as he caught himself on the edge of the bed. "Race you for the shower."

Henry followed, trying not to let his nerves sweep away the pleasure they'd just shared. More time with Jaden could never be a bad thing. Right?

Thirteen

HENRY

MAYBE JADEN REALLY *WAS* GETTING BETTER. HE WASN'T AFRAID to look out the car windows like he had been in Arizona. Every time he smiled at Henry, the knot of worry in Henry's chest eased.

Still, his unconscious body language told a different story. Getting from the building to Henry's car hadn't seemed like a big deal. But as they drove along the highway toward the mountains, Jaden started to tense up like a board.

Now he was jiggling his leg, sitting half-curled sideways as he looked at Henry more than the surroundings. It was a little unnerving to have Jaden stare as he drove, but he clearly needed the comfort.

So Henry reached out, taking Jaden's hand gently and resting their interlinked hands on the central console. "You all right?"

"Fine. Good. Perfect," Jaden responded with a quick, sharp laugh. His breathing was quick and shallow, like he was already winded from hiking.

"The more synonyms you use, the less I'll believe you," Henry warned him with a gentle smile.

That made Jaden giggle, at least. He took a deep breath and let it out. "Okay… not that great. But I'm out. It's a first step. A first step," he repeated under his breath with a firm nod.

"A great first step," Henry echoed with a smile. He tried not to pick up on Jaden's anxiety, and instead let it wash over him. The last thing he wanted was to reflect it back to him.

Jaden's determination never faltered, though. However anxious he was, it was clear to see that he wanted to push through. Henry was so proud of him; he just didn't know if it was the right thing to do.

The last thing he wanted to do was pressure Jaden into hurting himself. But he'd done all he could to let Jaden know that he didn't expect him to be over the phobia that had haunted him for years just because they'd met.

"I talked to my therapist this week. On the phone." Jaden seemed to be picking up on Henry's thoughts again. "She was so proud of me for wanting to try a hike before I get my support dog. She thinks I'm ready. But it will help when I have support. I mean, not that you aren't supportive." Jaden gave a tight little laugh.

Henry smiled. He sure as heck wanted to help, but he wasn't trained enough to do so. Any tool in Jaden's arsenal was a good one. "Oh yeah? When do you get the dog?"

"Next week." Jaden sounded excited, squeezing Henry's hand. "Her name's Cece. I drive there so they can make sure we're still working well together."

"Have you been waiting a long time for that?" Henry kept most of his attention on the road, flipping his hand palm-up in Jaden's grip.

His boyfriend started to trace the lines along Henry's palm. "Yeah. Months. Some people wait years. Just putting their lives on hold until then."

Henry whistled lowly. "Yeah. I know that feeling."

Jaden squeezed his fingers gently. "I bet. So yeah, I'm lucky. But it's really exciting." He sounded more animated now. "She'll be trained to help spot panic attacks and warn me, and look after me and help bring me out of them. And I can bring her most places. She's not trained as a service dog yet, so not *everywhere*, but… it'll help, at least."

Henry beamed at him. "That's awesome. Okay, we're nearly there."

All of a sudden, Jaden's easy confidence was gone. His eyes widened as he pressed himself back into his seat, looking like a deer in the headlights.

Henry swallowed hard as he pulled into the parking lot and found an empty space among the handful of cars already there. "How you doing now?" he finally asked once he was parked.

Jaden just wordlessly shook his head. Although Henry tried to grab his hand to give him a minute to recover, Jaden fumbled for his belt and practically flung himself out of the car.

"Shit," Henry muttered, shutting off the car and pocketing the keys, then getting out himself. By the time he got around to the other side, Jaden had his back flat against the vehicle, his eyes wide as he looked around.

The fresh air was wonderful—nothing like the city. And the vast peaks of the Rockies, gradually flattening into empty scrubland, healed Henry's soul. But he was well aware that Jaden might not feel the same way.

Henry came to stand next to him, not saying a word yet. Jaden took his hand in his own, but his grip was shaky.

Oh, poor guy. Henry hardly dared breathe, not wanting to shatter whatever internal negotiations were going on.

"This is… better than I thought," Jaden mumbled, still hardly blinking as he scanned the parking lot.

"I'm proud of you."

Then Henry made his biggest mistake: he leaned in to try to kiss Jaden's cheek.

Jaden choked and pushed at Henry's chest. The sinking, sickening lurch in his belly instantly reminded him what he'd done wrong. Jaden had never pushed Henry away like this.

But Jaden's gaze was glued to the car on the other side of the parking lot. It was surrounded by a mixed group of young people, maybe college aged. They were laughing loudly as they pulled off hiking boots and passed out cans of drinks.

Fuck. PDA. Henry winced and backed off, twisting his hands together. "Sorry," he breathed out, following his look. "They're cool, though, see?"

Jaden shot him a look that was clearly irritated. "They might not have been."

Henry bit his lip and nodded once, forcing himself to acknowledge that Jaden was right. He hadn't thought. He'd just gone ahead, loud and proud, when he knew better.

"You want me to give you space?" Henry asked instead, even though it was killing him. His chest was filled with knots at the idea of *not* touching Jaden to bring him back down and help ground him.

Jaden jerkily shook his head. "I want… I don't know."

"Tell you what," Henry murmured. He carefully put his hand on Jaden's arm to steer him toward the back of the car, then pulled open the door to the backseat. "If we get in there, nobody can see us."

"Oh," Jaden breathed out. Relief colored his voice. "Yes." He dropped into the seat heavily and scooted over, and Henry followed him inside and closed the door.

"Sorry," Henry murmured again, his cheeks burning.

Jaden shook his head. "No, I want… I *want* to be closer. In public. I want to be the guy I was five years ago." He slumped over, curling up in the middle seat and laying his head in Henry's lap.

Henry stroked his hair and shoulder gently, so relieved to get this moment with him. At least this seemed to be a safe place.

"I'm sorry I can't even get to the damn trailhead," Jaden mumbled, his hands twisted together and tucked under his chin. "Damn it, I thought I could at least do that."

"I startled you," Henry murmured, stroking the backs of his knuckles against Jaden's cheek. "That was my bad. But hey—you made it out of the house to my car. Then you made it for a whole drive here." He ticked both those things off on his fingers. "That's a lot for you, isn't it?"

"It is," Jaden admitted. The stiffness in his shoulders and voice was starting to subside. "Yeah. Yeah, it's good," he murmured, as if to himself. "And I'm safe here."

"You're always safe with me," Henry promised softly, his throat tight. God, how he wished he could jump back in time and be the one to say something—step in—help Jaden some-how. "But let's not push it when you're feeling bad, all right? We don't want to add bad experiences as evidence for your brain."

"Yeah." Jaden turned onto his back and smiled. "We can look at the view from here, right?"

"We sure can," Henry agreed, but the only view he was interested in was currently gazing up at him with a soft smile. He gently booped Jaden's nose.

Jaden giggled and swatted at his hand. "And—and when I get Cece, we can try again. That'll give me more time to get ready. But not so much time I get anxious about it."

"Perfect," Henry agreed softly.

He held Jaden for a long time in the back seat—past when Jaden tried to say he was fine, until he was really, truly fine.

Then they got in the front seat again for the drive home, and it was hard to miss the relief in Jaden's face when the car was moving again.

"I just wish you could hold me. All the time," Jaden murmured, giving him a little half-smile. "That helps a lot."

Henry's mind turned over this for a moment as he slowly nodded. "I have a crazy idea."

"Shoot." Jaden spoke in short sentences, but he didn't seem annoyed. He just seemed tired, like forming words was hard. And Henry couldn't blame him.

"Compression shirts? Have you heard of them?" Henry asked. When Jaden shook his head, he went on. "It's like a hug in jacket form—or leggings, or shirts, or whatever."

"Like yoga pants?"

"Something like that."

"What made you think of it?" Jaden asked. "Have you worn them?"

Henry cracked a grin. "In a way. I used to bind, before top surgery, right?"

"Oh. Duh." Jaden nodded.

"Well, after I finally got top surgery, I noticed I was... weirdly more anxious when I went out sometimes." Henry shrugged. "I didn't expect that. It's better now, though."

Jaden blinked at him. "You mean… surgery *didn't* help?"

"God, no. That's not it—believe me," Henry laughed.

That was an understatement. Just being able to do his job without meticulously planning how long he could be out, or what layers he could deal with wearing, or how long he could safely bind…

That wasn't even touching his own confidence, or how it felt to get undressed around people, or the *rightness* he felt when he touched his own chest.

He didn't think he could ever explain any of that adequately to Jaden.

"But I looked it up afterward, and I found compression vests for dogs who are afraid of thunderstorms, and then some vests and things for people who get sensory overload."

"Ohhh," Jaden breathed. He was sitting sideways again, his cheek against the headrest of the car seat. By now, Henry didn't mind Jaden watching him, though. It was kind of sweet. "Okay. Yeah, that's a good idea. I'll look it up."

"You'd have to be careful," Henry added firmly. "Not to wear them for too long or anything. I don't know how tight they are compared to binding, but I don't want you to hurt yourself while you're hiking."

"Right." Jaden hummed thoughtfully under his breath. "I'm doing okay here, in the car, though. I wonder if we could just go out driving more."

"We could do a road trip," Henry said with an easy grin. "I can get time off, no problem. I mean, I'm going to LA in a couple weeks to meet up with friends." Then he grimaced. "It's Santa Monica. The boardwalk. So I'll understand if you don't want to come right now."

His heart gave a nervous flip-flop. He'd never met Nic or any of his friends at the trans support group out there, but they'd invited him to their summer meeting and afternoon of fun.

Henry had always been worried that maybe he'd run into someone who knew him. But now... he wanted to push himself. And he *really* wanted to be around people who understood what he was going through as he left his own little bubble of safety—yet imprisonment.

He just didn't want to push Jaden too far yet.

"Hm." Jaden gazed out the window for a moment, tapping his fingers on his knee. His voice was soft and thoughtful, not the reckless tone he'd spoken in this morning. "I'll talk to Sandra and see what she thinks. It might be a good chance to... to get some closure on things."

"I can do the driving, in case you wanna hide out in the backseat or nap or anything," Henry offered. "It's a couple days' drive, so overnighting in Salt Lake City each way."

Henry worried that Cece might not be up for the road trip, but Jaden explained that part of her job would be going everywhere he did. By the time they'd worked out the details, Jaden actually sounded excited. Henry parked outside and walked Jaden through the dim entryway to the elevator, then all the way up to his apartment door and inside.

"Thank you," Jaden murmured once they made it. "I think I need to nap now. Sleep off everything. But... I want to do this again. Maybe with less panic."

Henry shook his head and kissed Jaden—this time, relief flooded his chest as Jaden melted into him and wrapped his arms around his neck. "It was my pleasure," he murmured back against those beautiful, soft lips. "I'll see you again soon, hm? Sleep well, hon."

Yet as Henry rattled around his own, much bigger house an hour or so later, it felt emptier than it ever had. More than anything, he wished he'd been able to bring Jaden home to his bed and tuck him in. That way, he could just pop upstairs and check on him.

One step at a time, Henry reminded himself, a smile touching his lips as he thought about what it had been like to wake up by Jaden's side.

And now they had a road trip to look forward to. This might go perfectly right—or terribly wrong. There was no way of knowing yet.

One thing was for sure: Henry was tired of hiding. He'd been lucky to get to live stealth for so long, and he didn't regret it for a minute. He'd learned everything about himself in that time. But now he couldn't deny that his carefully-constructed stories had gone from liberating to strangely claustrophobic.

Before Henry left for the Santa Monica meetup, he wanted to come out—at least to Trip.

Henry was ready for it; he'd been ready for years, in fact. He just hadn't realized until he'd met this brilliant, brave, beautiful man he could now call his boyfriend.

No matter what happened, he trusted Jaden to be by his side. And that in itself was a miracle.

CHAPTER

Fourteen

JADEN

"CECE, SIT."

Jaden almost trembled as Sandra passed him the leash. His therapist was in her late forties, with a kind smile that he didn't get to see in their phone appointments.

Today was the big day; Jaden had come into her office to meet her—and his new emotional support dog, along with her trainer, Neil.

As his hand wrapped around the thick cloth of Cece's leash, she sat patiently, craning her neck to look around at everyone else.

Oh my God, I have a dog now.

"Say hi to her," Sandra encouraged Jaden gently. Neil looked on, hands in his pockets, his expression a mix of pride and sorrow.

Who could blame him? Neil had trained Cece in the basic commands for the last two months and assessed her suitability to work as a psychiatric service dog.

Now Cece was ready to be considered an emotional support animal while Jaden finished her training in the tasks that would qualify her as a service dog. She had to learn to recognize his panic attacks, to apply deep pressure therapy, and to block people approaching him too closely.

Until then, she didn't have the same rights, so Jaden's independence was on the line.

It would be a steep learning curve for them both, even with Neil's help completing her training. But Jaden was determined to do it—for the sake of his whole future.

More than anything, he wanted to just go to the grocery store or the bank without planning it for three days in advance. To be able to hike with his boyfriend without melting down in the parking lot. To live a normal life.

"Hi, sweetie." Jaden was stiff as he bent over, the compression shirt not quite the usual comfortable T-shirt he lived in when he was at home. But the pressure had helped get him here—like Henry had said, it was kind of like a hug. Not as rib-crushing as a binder, though.

Jaden knelt in front of the golden retriever, burying his face in her fur as he hugged her closely. She sat still, recognizing that she had to behave while her vest was on.

"Good," Neil said softly. "I'm confident she'll behave—as long as you remember everything I've taught you."

Jaden had met Cece here at his therapist's office a few times before, and he'd talked to Neil on the phone about what to expect. Now there would be a lot more in-person meetings with him to establish the tasks she needed to perform.

Let's get through it together, he thought, letting go of Cece and scratching her head as her tongue lolled happily.

"Thank you," Jaden murmured from his crouch, looking up at Neil. Then he smiled at Sandra, who had recommended Neil as a trainer and friend who had helped some of her other clients. And she'd helped him get a grant to afford Neil's training.

So few people in Jaden's shoes got this far—most ended up with an emotional support dog that couldn't even accompany them to the places they most needed help.

This was the opportunity of a lifetime. Jaden didn't want to let it slip past him.

So he straightened up and took Cece's leash with a deep breath.

"I'll see you tomorrow," he told Neil with a confident nod. They were going to meet at the dog park to go over the basics yet again—more for Jaden's benefit than Cece's.

It was the most structure he'd had to his week in years. This past week, Henry had come over every few days with groceries. Spence had visited once, but he'd been visibly relieved when Jaden told him the big news: that Henry was his boyfriend now.

He's glad I have someone else to rely on so he can get on with his life. Jaden knew it was fair, but it still stung. And it made him bristle. He was *not* just going to rely on Henry from now on instead of Spence.

"Yep. Tomorrow it is. Good luck with her." Neil gave the two of them a brisk nod and strode out of the room.

Sandra smiled after him and then looked back at them. "And I'm just a call away, if you need anything." It was her lunch break, so she didn't even have to do this... but she was going out of her way to support him in this transition to a very different life than he'd hid away in for these last few years.

Jaden offered a shaky smile as his grip tightened on the leash. "Okay. Thanks. Talk to you soon." *Hopefully not before our next scheduled appointment,* he added mentally.

"Come, Cece."

She obediently stood and followed him to the elevator, staying at his heel.

The familiar trudge through the parking garage flew by, he was so distracted watching her. It took him until he got to the car before it really sank in: this was it. He was going to have to get out of the house every day now—multiple times a day. Even if it was just to the grassy scrubby lawn behind the apartment building so she could relieve herself.

Before embarking on this whole journey, he'd thought it through, of course. But it wasn't the same as this moment actually coming in real life, at last.

Wow. It was overwhelming, but not in the bad way he'd expected. More... a new way.

"Load up, girl," he urged, opening the back passenger door of the car. She climbed into the footwell and then hopped up onto the seat so Jaden could attach the brand-new car harness to her vest.

Careful of her tail, he shut the door. By the time he climbed into the driver's seat, she was lying attentively on the backseat, tail wagging slightly.

"Yes, you're adorable," Jaden told her, smiling to himself as he started the car. "But you're not coming up here."

He wanted to make sure she wouldn't lunge for him in the event of a panic attack while driving. There was a lot more to come in her training, and they barely knew each other yet.

"Whew," Jaden breathed out, rubbing his face. "Let's do this, Cece. It's you and me versus the world, huh? Well... you, me, and Henry. You'll meet him today."

As he drove, Jaden kept chatting to Cece. Even if she couldn't understand, it was nice to have the distraction.

Between explaining how he'd met Henry and driving, they were home before he knew it.

As he parked, he waited for her to sit up and then snapped a selfie over his shoulder, grinning for the camera.

"Unload," he told her, carefully using the word they'd chosen as she jumped down.

While he waited for the elevator, Jaden texted Henry the photo of the two of them.

Look who's home!!!!!

The response was almost instant.

OMG! Can I come over right now???

Jaden giggled at Henry's enthusiastic message, which was followed by several heart-eye emojis.

Come on over :)

The elevator arrived at his floor, so he led Cece out. "Heel, girl," he said, unlocking the apartment door. "And… we're home."

The tour didn't last long, but he made sure to show her the new dog bed, all the new toys, the food and water dishes… *God, if this is expensive, no kids for me*, Jaden thought, chuckling to himself.

Once Jaden wriggled out of his compression shirt and back into his regular T-shirt, he unclipped Cece's vest.

"Release," he told her, grinning. She deserved some time off and praise. "Up."

There was no point in trying to keep her off the couch. She was going to have to apply deep pressure therapy once she was trained to do so, no matter where he was.

Cece jumped up beside him, then whined and wriggled into his lap on the couch.

"That's right," Jaden smiled at her, scratching her belly.

"Hello there, girl. We're gonna be an awesome team, aren't we? Yes, we are."

The pressure on his lap already soothed him from the exhausting experience of another trip outdoors. It made him breathe a deep sigh of relief—but better yet, hope.

Jaden rested with Cece on the couch, falling into an easy rhythm of stroking her soft fur as he closed his eyes. It seemed like just moments later that there was a knock on the door.

Cece barked once and jumped to the floor, but then she sat and looked at him.

"Good girl," Jaden praised. Even with her harness off, she wasn't supposed to cause mayhem every time someone knocked on a door. "Sit. Stay."

He tried to walk calmly to the door so he didn't encourage her to run after him, but it was hard. By the time he got there, Jaden was wriggling with more excitement than Cece.

"Hi!" Jaden exclaimed as he pulled open the door.

Henry stepped inside and set a bag down. Then, he swept Jaden off his feet and planted a kiss on his lips. "*Helloooo* there, handsome."

Jaden giggled and batted at Henry's chest. "Put me down, you brute."

"Right away. As soon as I take care of important, outstanding business." Henry pressed Jaden against the wall and kissed him again, softly, before kicking the door shut. Then he returned to the important business.

His lips were soft and wet, and the musk of him made Jaden go a little dizzy. When Henry set Jaden on his feet again, he leaned on his boyfriend for a moment, his knees weak.

"Jesus. I'm going to invite you over multiple times a day if you keep that up."

"That's the secret plan," Henry winked at him. "So, where's this supposed hound?"

"Sitting and waiting like a very good girl." Jaden beamed and took Henry by the hand to lead him to the living room. "This is Henry," he told Cece. The two of them sat on the couch. "Up, girl. Come meet him."

"Cece? What a beauty!" Henry gasped, scratching her ruff and kissing the top of her head. "Oh, she's too sweet." Then he glanced at Jaden. "She *is* off-duty, right?"

"Yes. Don't worry," Jaden assured Henry with a smile, squeezing his knee.

Henry breathed a sigh of relief. "Phew. Glad I didn't instantly fuck up. Give it time. Don't listen to Uncle Henry's filthy mouth, darling," he added, scratching her as she gazed adoringly at him.

Well, they were getting along like a house on fire already. Jaden laughed and shook his head, watching his new dog bonding with his new boyfriend.

For a moment, it felt like... they were a family unit. All three of them against the world.

That was crazy. It was way too soon. None of them were ready for that yet. Right?

Distracted by his thoughts, it took Jaden a minute to notice her signals. "Oh, I think she needs to go out." Cece cocked her head and looked interested. "Let's see," Jaden said and stood up. "You can wait here if you want."

"Nah. I came here to see you." Henry stood up, his eyes bright.

Jaden snorted with laughter. "Not in an overgrown field watching the dog go potty."

"Wherever you go, I go. Well… not literally." Henry's lips twitched into a grin. "Unless you're into that."

Jaden shook his head. "Well, that's a discussion to have someday," he laughed.

It took all his focus to use the right words as commanded Cece to heel as he clipped her leash back on. This time, she just had her collar. He twitched two fingers at Henry, signaling him to follow.

"So all those words mean different things?" Henry asked as they got into the elevator.

"Yep. And I have to keep them all straight," Jaden said with a sheepish grin. "Or I'll undo weeks of training."

Henry whistled and shook his head, holding the elevator door once they arrived. He followed the others out. "She won't listen to me, though, right? I don't have to be careful not to say…" He looked at her askance. "Like, c-o-m-e. When we're… you know… right at an inconvenient moment…"

Jaden burst out laughing. It was all he could do not to stumble as he led Cece out to the side of the building. He could hardly even look at Henry with the mental image in his brain.

"Get busy, Cece," Jaden commanded. When he recovered his composure, Jaden finally managed to look at his boyfriend again. "No, I think we'll be fine, as long as you aren't shouting her name, too."

"Oh, God. I hope I'm not. If I am, it'll be *get out and close the door behind you, please*," Henry said, grinning as he took Jaden's hand.

And Jaden didn't mind the touch. With Cece's leash curled around his fingers and Henry by his other side, he felt… okay out here.

On their way back into the building, they bumped into

Ron, the grumpy middle-aged live-in property manager. Jaden resisted a sigh and roll of his eyes when the guy side-eyed them like they were robbing the place.

"Thanks," Jaden said pointedly when the guy didn't hold the door for them.

He just grunted back and took the stairwell door with another long, hard stare out of the corner of his eye.

Henry raised an eyebrow and looked at Jaden. "Um… neighbor issues?"

"Property manager. He lives right below me. Even when I had a busted shower and he accompanied the plumber, he hardly looked at me." Jaden rolled his eyes. "Probably thinks I'm a camboy since I never leave the apartment."

"And you're insanely pretty," Henry followed up without missing a beat, grinning when Jaden's cheeks flushed. "Aw. And you blush easily, too."

"Stop that," Jaden hissed and smacked Henry's chest, but he couldn't hide his laugh.

"Complimenting you? Never, sweetheart." Henry hit the button for Jaden's floor and beamed at him. "I can't believe anyone doesn't want to stare at you all day."

Jesus, Jaden's cheeks were on fire. He bit his lip and squirmed, his breathing suddenly shallow and quick.

Cece immediately wriggled between them, leaning against Jaden's leg with a little whine. They both laughed, Henry gave a shrug of defeat and mock woeful pout as he held the elevator for Jaden again.

"Oh, no. I have a rival for your heart… and your bed." Henry crowded up behind Jaden and nibbled his ear.

"I know which of you is more of a nuisance," Jaden scolded fondly. He unlocked his apartment door and set

Cece off her lead, then ushered Henry in before he shut it. "But never. There's room for you both."

Henry winked at him and pulled him in for another kiss while Cece was busy finding her water bowl. "We'll find out tonight."

Why did Jaden have the feeling *he* was going to end up with a sliver of the bed? And why did the thought fill him with an even warmer glow than the blush that still faded on his cheeks?

Maybe they *were* already becoming a family unit. Jaden wanted that—more than anything.

Fifteen

HENRY

IT WAS TIME. WAY PAST TIME, IN FACT—BUT THE LAST FEW years had never quite given Henry the confidence he'd needed.

He was crouching on the shore of the river, washing out supper dishes and packing the kayaking gear he'd left to dry. That gave him far too much time to think.

Being with Jaden had made Henry see things differently. It was hard not to draw parallels to his own coming-out. Nobody had been able to take away the hard parts of what he'd been through in his transition, but having loved ones by his side gave him a foundation he could always depend on.

He wanted to be that foundation for Jaden. And he wanted his own taste of freedom. No more avoiding talking about his childhood. No more dancing around questions about his scars. No more comparing himself to other guys, making sure he was *doing it right*.

Like his transness was something to disown and shove into a box and put away. Some people could be happy living that way—but that wasn't Henry. But he also wasn't the kind of person who wanted to tell *everyone* his life story. Finding a balance was going to be the hard part.

I can start small, he reminded himself. *No need to tell the world. Just Trip at first.*

So why did it feel scarier to tell his best friend than someone he didn't even know? An uncomfortable squirm in his stomach reminded him: because Trip might not treat him the same as he always had anymore. And that would hurt so badly.

But if he let these fears keep holding him back, Henry would just stay safe in his little cocoon—the bubble that had quietly, without any great fanfare, solidified into an iron cage.

It was a risk for other reasons, too. Of course it was. Just because it was *technically* illegal to discriminate against him didn't mean people would listen. And it didn't matter how much he loved and accepted himself if the wrong person thought his past was their business.

But Henry was tired of letting assholes dictate the terms of his life—his silence in exchange for some limited freedoms. Freedom with terms and conditions attached wasn't really freedom. If the idea of freedom existed at all.

What the fuck was a guy supposed to do?

"Can I give you a hand?"

Henry lurched and nearly went face-first into the river.

Beck lunged for his shoulder and grabbed him to pull him back as he laughed. "Sorry!"

Henry shook his head. "No, man. My bad." He shouldn't get so lost in his thoughts while he had a group to take care of.

Beck was every inch a bear—middle-aged, with a big

fuzzy belly and a smile that warmed his face up instantly. "Lots on your mind?"

He was one of their frequent guests. He'd been in different gay camping groups several times before with Henry, and Henry respected him. He always listened and never complained.

"Yeah, you could say that." Henry offered a sheepish smile as he got his balance on his toes again. "Thanks. If you could grab those bags, I gotta carry all this stuff back."

"No problem." Beck swung the backpacks on his shoulders with ease. "You all right?"

"Oh, yeah. Yeah." Henry's mouth was dry and his palms were damp all of a sudden.

Maybe this can be a test run. Henry could hardly breathe, but he did his best to sound casual. "Just thinking about the closet, and freedom, and all kinds of gay shit that keeps me awake." He managed a laugh that he thought sounded carefree.

Judging by the concerned look Beck gave him, his attempt at levity missed the mark. "Ouch. That sounds heavy." Beck adjusted the straps and looked him over. "Something you wanna talk about, or something you wanna forget about? I have homemade flavored vodka. It's great for the latter."

"You're my new favorite," Henry told him with a light grin, his steps slowing as they approached the campsite.

The other three guys were lounging around, enamel cups in hand. One talked with enthusiastic gestures and waves while the other two laughed. Nobody would miss them for a minute.

Beck clutched his chest like he was honored. "I'll tell them you said so. Incessantly."

But despite the banter between them, Henry sensed that Beck was waiting—giving him the chance to talk, if he wanted to.

"Well, I…" Oh, God. He might actually be sick if he made himself say the words.

Henry hadn't expected it to grow and grow inside him until it felt like a secret. It *wasn't* a secret. And it sure as hell wasn't anything anybody else was entitled to know.

But now it felt like a great big cloud inside him.

"I met a guy." Henry blinked, half-surprised at the way it came out without his bidding. *Was* that where he wanted to start? Too late now.

"Uh huh…" Beck gave him a knowing nod.

Thinking of Jaden made Henry smile, which made the knot in his chest ease. "And he's really brave, and gorgeous, and all that mushy stuff. And it makes me want to… do everything I was always afraid to do."

"Hey! Guys, last bag of marshmallows." Jonny waved a skewer in their direction.

"Oh, hell yeah!" Beck called back. He started walking toward the fire pit, glancing at Henry.

Ah, crap, Henry thought. Now he had to either drop the conversation or come out to all of them at once. But he fixed a nervous smile on his face and stayed by Beck's side.

"Sounds like love. What's the holdup?" Beck asked. "Is he in the closet?"

Jonny perked up as the other two guys, Art and Inigo, turned their heads. "What's this about a closet?" Jonny asked.

Oh, fuck me. Henry felt the blood drain from his cheeks. Fear kept his jaw stiff as he sat on the log opposite their small cooking fire.

The scary part wasn't disclosing his past, exactly. He

could just stop now. He didn't have to say anything. He could just move on with the conversation and forget about it.

It was only scary because he found himself *wanting* to talk about it, for the first time in so many years. Like a pebble shifting in the foundation of a mountain, things were no longer simple.

It wasn't easy to go stealth—he'd lost most of his friends who'd known him in middle school and earlier, moved to a new high school. But never telling anyone made for simple choices.

Now he had to think about who he trusted and why he didn't or did want to tell people, and all of that was exposing things he thought he'd gotten past long ago.

"Sounds like Henry's got boy problems," Beck told them, prompting Henry with a nod.

"No," Henry said quickly, and then tipped his head back and laughed. "Actually, yes, in a way." God, his inside joke was about to become an outside joke. "He's not closeted. I am. Sort of."

Beck looked startled but didn't say anything. He took a skewer and a marshmallow.

Henry's eyes fell to the skewer being offered to him. For half a moment, he imagined the damage it could do. *Oh, come on*, he told himself a moment later, shaking his head as he accepted one. *They're cool. That's why I'm talking to them.* All four of them had only been open-minded, happy-go-lucky, and they respected Henry's teaching and guidance.

But it was hard not to imagine the worst outcomes.

"Yeah?" Jonny prompted. None of the guys said much now, just turning their skewers as they held the sugary treats close to the embers.

And waited. For Henry to say something. He had to. It was now or never.

"I'm trans," Henry said, the words coming so much faster than he'd thought they would. His ears rang and his hands shook. Somehow he was very aware of the texture of the marshmallow, grainy yet soft on his palm, as he pushed it onto the skewer.

"Oh," Beck said softly, no doubt realizing why Henry had struggled to explain. Inigo and Jonny exchanged confused looks, like they weren't quite sure what he meant.

They were probably assuming that he was a trans woman, like most people did, so Henry hurried to explain before they could congratulate him for the wrong reasons.

"I transitioned like, ten years ago. It was amazing, leaving my past behind. Everyone in my life knows the real me now. But..." Henry trailed off, clearing his throat. "It's started to feel like this thing that I hide from people, and I don't like that. As if it's a bad thing, or a secret. And it's *not*. But I didn't know what to do about it until I met this guy, and... oh, Jesus." Henry laughed, the knot of fear in his chest disintegrating into butterflies. "You guys are the first people I've told aside from him and a couple doctors since I was like, twenty-one."

"Well, uh, I wasn't expecting that." Beck reached around the fire, his fist held out. As Henry, still dazed, bumped his knuckles against Beck's, the big, friendly bear smiled. "Kudos to you, man," he said.

"Yeah. That takes guts." Jonny stood up and came around the fire to sit next to Henry, putting an arm around his shoulders. "Thanks for telling us."

"How does it feel?" Art asked as Inigo nodded.

Jesus, how could he explain it? Henry remembered what

it was like to breathe, his cheeks flushing with embarrassment at everyone watching him.

"Like coming out all over again. It's weird," Henry said, the tension slowly draining from him. "I keep thinking I should be glad that I can pass." He made a face and air-quoted around the word. He'd always hated it, and what it stood for. "But it's not the magic bullet I thought it was."

"No. I guess it's kind of like being bi. You can pass as straight or gay, but you're always hiding a part of yourself if you do," Jonny said quietly, his chin propped on his fist, elbow on his knee. "So how liberating is that, really?"

That made sense. A lot of sense, actually. Henry perked up and nodded. "Yeah—" he started and then caught sight of his marshmallow.

While he was distracted by their conversation, the skewer had dipped too low. Now flames were licking up the sugary treat, scorching the outside.

"Oh, shit," Henry laughed, scrambling to his feet as he pulled his new torch out of the fire and blew on it frantically.

The other guys burst out laughing, whooping with laughter at his expense.

"Put it out in Beck's cup," Jonny offered, grabbing it.

"No, you asshole." Beck grabbed it back and kicked him.

It was hard to blow out the marshmallow while he was laughing, but Henry eventually managed it. He sank down again and shrugged. "Lesson learned. Don't get distracted while roasting marshmallows." At least he didn't mind burned foods. Too many nights learning to cook over campfires had taught him to eat anything, really.

The others gasped and groaned as he pulled it off the skewer and let the charred remains melt over his tongue. The sweet, sticky inside of the marshmallow eventually helped wash away the burnt taste, but Henry grabbed the cup they put in his hand and swigged anyway.

Strawberry vodka. Nice, but strong. So now his throat and tongue burned all over again, and his taste buds were screaming with the collision of flavors.

I might never taste anything again, Henry lamented.

Jonny clapped Henry's back as he coughed and stuck out his tongue. "Oh, Jesus. I don't know if that's better or worse," Henry managed.

"Can't be worse, my recipes are flawless," Beck informed him. Everyone made skeptical noises in response.

Eventually Henry found the water and chugged enough that he could think straight again. He shook his head when Jonny offered him the bag. "I think I've had enough dessert for now."

Everyone grinned and settled in again, but the laughter had helped chase out any lingering tension and doubts.

Now Henry felt good. He was able to just bask in the moment, instead of planning and second-guessing himself and thinking up worst-case scenarios.

"I'm glad I said something," Henry finally said as the campfire dwindled away to nothing. "I've been sitting on that for a long time. And it feels good."

Beck nodded. "I don't know what it's like on that side of the fence. But I know that if you're carrying around other people's shame, you don't have room for your own joy. Glory. Even freedom."

Silence fell for a few moments as they all turned the words over in their heads.

I guess I was carrying around other people's shame, Henry thought. *Trans people's, cis people's, it doesn't matter. A lot of*

*people would rather I just kept my mouth shut and fit into a box,
even if it's not the same box they thought I was born into.*

Henry wanted to put that box down and make room in
his life for other things. Like Jaden, and their future together.
For the first time, he felt like he could be his whole, unapologetic self with someone and they'd only love him more for it.

Henry sipped his water again, letting it roll over his
tongue. It was almost like whisky if he pretended that was
where the lingering smoky taste came from.

"There's always joy at a free glory hole." Art's cheerful
comment made everyone, including Henry, break into
groans.

Inigo elbowed him. "That was a perfectly nice moment
and you ruined it, man. God. Why do I put up with you?"

"Because I know my free glory holes, duh."

Henry laughed and sprawled back against his log and
looked up at the sky, and the stars that seemed warm and
welcoming now.

Jaden was going to be so proud tomorrow. Henry would
tell him in the car, when they hit the road for their three-night
trip to LA and their pasts—or future, he couldn't tell which.

But his gut told him that he was going the right direction
again. And if he'd listened to one thing in his life, that had
been it. It had never been wrong yet.

Everything was going to be okay.

The spark of confidence that had carried Henry straight into
the Blue Skies headquarters was starting to flicker.

It was one thing to tell a bunch of guests he only saw a

few times a year. It was quite another to talk to his best friend and coworker—the guy he saw every day, laughed around with, and relied on to keep him safe.

But Trip was in there on the couch, surrounded by release forms and sorting them into envelopes. "Oh, hey," he greeted with a grin. "How'd everything go?"

"Good." Henry nodded and shoved his hands into his pockets. "But I want to tell you something."

"Yeah?" Trip rubbed a hand down his bristly face, looking curious. "What's that?"

"I've been… holding onto this one for a long time." Henry gave a shaky little laugh. "With everyone in my life. And I'm tired of it."

"Dude, I know you're gay," Trip said with a teasing grin, but he cleared away the papers next to him and patted the couch.

Henry gave him a grateful nod and sat down. "Well, I'm trans, too." He took a deep breath, trying to give Trip a moment to let that sink in. But it didn't work. His anxiety made his mouth keep going even as his brain tried to reel it in. "That's why I've had time off for so many surgeries. And why I was so worried about going on a date before I met Jaden."

"Oh." A slow smile spread over Trip's face. "I'm really glad you told me. Thanks, man."

Henry groaned with relief as Trip pulled him in for a hug. Yet he was suspicious. Something about the way Trip reacted was almost too casual. "You knew, didn't you?"

Trip looked guilty when Henry pulled away from the hug. "Yeah. I guessed," he admitted. "But I knew you had your own reasons for not wanting to talk about it, and I didn't want to put you on the spot."

"Jesus," Henry muttered, laughing and pinching his nose. "Here I was, winding myself up into knots about this all week."

He'd only done it now, right before the road trip, in case Trip came out of left field and had a big problem with it. Then he'd at least have a few days to cool off.

"No, it's fine." Trip squeezed his shoulder. "It's your choice whether you want people to know. And it's gotta be scary."

"A little." Henry smiled at him as the weight lifted from his chest. "I didn't want to tell you at first because I thought being trans was something I'd leave behind. Like it was just who I *was*. For some people, it works that way. But not me. Meeting Jaden made me finally realize that I'm not me *in spite of* being trans. It's still a big part of who I am. I want to own it, just like I own being gay." He was smiling by the time he finished speaking, his heart soaring. It felt so much better to get it out there.

"And being a giant dork." Trip grinned and shoved him lightly. "Telling me now when I can't take you out to Buckle to celebrate. When do you leave?"

"Tomorrow, but I'm staying over at his place tonight," Henry admitted, laughing. "When I get back, though?"

"You bet." Trip smiled. "This doesn't change anything. But thank you for trusting me. That means a lot."

This time it was Henry who hugged Trip tightly.

They were both laughing and bantering like usual by the time Henry stood up.

The office door opened, and Henry's gut did a funny swoop as Damien came out, walkie-talkies in hand. He glanced at Trip, who widened his eyes and shrugged. He hadn't known Damien was here either, then.

Shit. Did he hear us?

Henry's stomach tightened and nausea rose in his belly. He hadn't told Damien why he was off for surgery—and Damien had carefully never asked, knowing perfectly well that he wasn't allowed.

But he'd always made it clear that he wasn't happy about Henry's time off. He'd settled on aggressively wishing Henry a swift recovery after each surgery.

Just as his gut had told him that his guests were going to be okay, and Trip would be more than accepting… it also warned him not to broach the subject with his boss.

Technically, because they were in Colorado, Henry's job was safe. But 'technically' meant nothing if Damien had decided to be transphobic. There were plenty of ways to drive someone out of a job.

"Oh, hey. Henry, you're here." Damien sounded distracted as he fiddled with the gear. "Are you taking off now?"

"Yeah. I'll be back next week," Henry said. His chest was tight again. Was he overthinking this, or was Damien not looking at him? "See you Monday."

"SoCal, right? Have a good time. Trip, I'm going to throw these fucking things out the window if you can't get them working."

Henry bit his lip as he tried to lay his worries to rest. He knew Trip wouldn't out him, but Damien was impossible to read right now. It *sounded* like Damien hadn't heard, but who knew?

"Have a great time," Trip told him. "Enjoy your weekend of freedom."

"Oh, I plan to." Henry raised a hand for a wave and strode out of the cabin, trying to ignore the rain clouds of uncertainty that now threatened the briefly clear skies of his mind.

CHAPTER
Sixteen

JADEN

When was the last time Jaden had been on a real road trip?

It had to have been with Spence. Maybe on his way to the first year of college? Things had been so different back then. His big brother had still looked after him, but not the way he'd had to in recent years.

I want that again, Jaden thought as he gazed out the window, his feet up on the dashboard, fidgeting with a cold iced tea bottle.

He wanted that relationship—where he and Spence could just screw around and make fun of each other and do cool shit without Spence feeling responsible for him.

And he was making progress. Spence had come over yesterday for an hour or so, just to catch up on things and talk. The air seemed to be clearing between them.

Plus, Spence had let slip that he had a girlfriend now. Jaden was happy for him. He deserved to make plans and move forward with his life.

And Jaden? He was doing pretty damn well for himself.

They were close to the beach now, after two days of driving and one night in a cheap little Utah hotel. The vest on Cece had quieted the clerk's complaint. And they'd ignored one of the beds and slept together on the other.

It was nice and normal and above all, addictively fun. Nothing whatsoever of note had happened, and yet Jaden stored the details from this road trip like precious mementoes.

The gas stops, the drive-through burgers, the game of spotting yellow cars.

It was all so delightfully ordinary, yet wildly adventurous compared to Jaden's last few years. And every laugh he shared with Henry about a silly little joke they'd forget in a few minutes' time brought them closer together than ever.

It was *easy* to be around Henry. Jaden wasn't on show or on guard.

"Hey, Cece. Are you going to have any of that bear left by the time we get there?" Henry grinned as he pointed to the rearview mirror.

When Jaden turned around, he groaned. She was off-duty, clipped into the backseat, and she'd managed to gnaw her way through the other arm of the poor teddy bear.

"She's a menace," Henry said with a chuckle. "No respect for that bear. We'll have to see if we can get her another from somewhere…"

Jaden grinned at him. "In the very same sentence, you're already spoiling her. But I think we found our serial killer all along. Hey, that's what we should call her instead of Cecilia."

She cocked her head and looked up when he said her name.

"Serial Killer? You definitely can't yell that at the dog park." Henry laughed. "How about Cereal?"

"That's... not a bad idea. It's close enough, I think," Jaden said with a grin. "She should recognize it."

"And her fur looks like Frosted Flakes." Henry smiled. "Cereal. I like it."

Cece woofed, low in her throat. Clearly she'd decided she was about to be given a command.

"It's okay," Jaden said with a chuckle, reaching back to scratch her ears until she settled. "We'll be out of the car soon."

"Very soon, in fact." Henry patted Jaden's knee. "Legs down, please. We're coming into town. And you know that's not safe."

Jaden stuck out his tongue but wiggled in his seat until his feet were down. "Fine, spoilsport. Here was me, giving you a good view."

"A very distracting good view," Henry countered, winking at him. "Help me find parking first, though."

They were heading straight to the boardwalk and going their separate ways for the afternoon—Jaden and Cece for a walk on their own, and Henry to meet his online friends. Then they'd crash in a hotel here for the night before another long day of driving.

Henry didn't seem to mind, though. He actually seemed to relax and light up while driving, much like he had outdoors. Though as they approached the city, Henry had grown noticeably more restless.

Once they'd finally found a spot, reality sank in. It was time to do this. Way, *way* too late to turn back.

As Henry climbed out of the car and stretched, Jaden kept himself busy. He had to get both himself and Cece out of the car safely, following her training commands.

That helped until he got to the edge of the parking lot. Then he stopped, his heart rising into his throat.

"Are you okay?" Henry murmured, hovering close to Jaden but not quite touching.

Jaden took his hand and nodded, squeezing once before letting go. "Yeah. Sandra knows what's happening. And I won't be alone, because I have Cece. But I need to do this myself."

Plus, he didn't want to keep Henry from meeting his online friends.

"Okay," Henry said slowly. He seemed to be trying to stall, like maybe *he* was nervous, too. It was weirdly nice not to be the only one who was worried.

"Okay," Jaden echoed in a whisper.

Henry drew a breath and let it out, stretching and patting down his pockets for at least the third time. "Text me if you need anything at all."

"You, too," Jaden told him. Adrenaline rushed through him, quickening his breath and heart rate as he clutched the leash on Cece's vest a little tighter.

I want to do this, he reminded himself fiercely. He'd planned it all day today. Right here of all places, so close to the spot where his life had broken down... it was perfect.

It felt anything but perfect.

Before Henry could step away, Jaden caught his hand and stretched up onto his toes to kiss him.

It was just a peck on the lips—casual, light, fun. But the fear that roiled his gut was not. Years of therapy had taught him to identify it as his lizard brain response. To point out to himself the irrationality of his thoughts.

But that didn't stop them pouring in, and above them all

the one thought that repeated like a drumbeat: *Don't attract danger!*

Henry looked startled, his eyes flying wide open as an adorable blush spread across his cheeks. It took a moment before he recovered his wits enough to kiss Jaden back.

When Jaden pulled away, Cece leaned against his leg. His hand went into the ruff of her fur, and he took a few deep breaths to ground himself. "There," Jaden murmured when he was sure that he was okay.

"Cece knows you're pushing yourself," Henry said with a gentle smile at her.

"Yeah. And I'll listen to her," Jaden promised softly. "So… see you this evening." They'd arranged to meet in front of the famous outdoor gym. Jaden had giggled that he needed a photo of Henry outflexing the statue of the ridiculously muscled guy.

"See you this evening, sweetie," Henry told him. He looked less unhappy to be leaving Jaden now, raising a hand for a cheery wave and striding off.

That left Jaden alone—but not alone. Cece was right there with him, sitting and gazing up at him.

"Let's go," he told her softly, and she got to her feet, ready to stay at his side.

It didn't take him long to find the spot. Most days, for at least a moment, he thought about the boardwalk. And his nightmares—mercifully, less frequent now—dragged him unwillingly to this place and back in time.

Stalls were set up on the pavement to one side, shops on the other. The brightly painted buildings that had haunted his memories like a funhouse nightmare were just… average. The musicians selling CDs were no longer pointing and laughing like they did in Jaden's dreams.

The sidewalk was dusty, the sky was vividly blue, and a crowd of people in shorts and sandals strolled past the tourist trap of a memento shop that Jaden and his now-ex had once run into, frantic with fear.

Jaden's steps slowed as he reached the spot. It was anticlimactic, standing here with Cece by his side while people walked around them.

Everyone was blissfully unaware of what this spot meant to Jaden. The threads of memories he'd held for so long, that had wrapped themselves around him until they constricted the life out of him, and him out of his own life, had felt like they must be engraved on this place.

Like somehow, the center of all his unhappiness couldn't be sunny and bright. People couldn't laugh nearby or hold hands—that stung the most, watching couples walk by with no idea how easy it was for them.

Jaden's mind raced, and yet it felt strangely empty. All the anxious thoughts about this place being some kind of harbinger of danger... felt hollow.

Life was going on as normal right now, flowing past this place like it was nothing.

And nothing was exactly what happened. Jaden stood here, and the palm trees overhead rustled softly with the ocean breeze, and the skateboarders whooshed past him with irritated sighs.

To him, that *nothing* was everything.

Jaden's chest swelled as his tight breathing finally eased. This spot *was* nothing. Jaden was so much more—so much stronger—than one asshole he'd never see again. Two, if he counted his now-ex.

It wasn't fair, what he'd done, leaving Jaden on his own to cope. Moving away, ghosting him. Everyone coped how they had to, but blaming Jaden? Leaving him without a word? No. That was a dick move, and Jaden deserved better.

He *had* better, now. He had Henry.

Jaden finally led Cece to the side so he wasn't right in the middle of the thoroughfare. He scratched her head and closed his eyes. What was Henry doing right now? Watching him get all cutely nervous about meeting his online friends was so sweet. Were they already getting along well?

Jaden hoped so. He was nervous for Henry, but excited, too. Henry had talked to him so much on the way here about transition and his life since then. It sounded like he'd gone through much of it alone—without other trans people who understood and had been there, too.

It didn't take him long to find a spot where he could sit and people-watch, but he kept his back to the wall. He was already asking enough of his brain—he didn't need to push it further.

Everything was so much better than Jaden had ever anticipated. He hadn't tipped over that edge, past fearful and nervous, into flat-out disbelief.

Even though he was here, at the epicenter of the quake that had shaken his life apart—at the fault line that ran through the middle of his world. The ghosts of his past were silent. It was just another spot on the sidewalk.

Jaden let out his breath and leaned over to hug Cece to him again, burying his face in her fur. "Good girl," he whispered.

He knew perfectly well this wasn't going to fix anything miraculously. He'd still have to fight his instincts to hold Henry's hand, and to walk through crowds without watching his back. He'd have to push himself out the door some days, and run back home other days. He had weeks of training Cece and months of therapy still ahead of him.

But for the first time, Jaden let the years behind him really sink in. They *were* behind him.

For today, he was okay.

CHAPTER

Seventeen

HENRY

The group of half-a-dozen trans guys had already wandered up and down the boardwalk a little bit, getting corndogs and coffee and deep-fried Ding Dongs. One of them, Jake, knew this little hole-in-the-wall cheap place for great coffee. Then they'd found a comfier spot in the sand where they could talk more openly.

"I'm so glad we finally got to meet!" Nic, the leader of the support group, was sitting next to Henry. He was a bit shorter, with gelled hair and a warm smile.

Nic was different than Henry had pictured him, even from seeing photos in their mutual Facebook groups. They couldn't be more opposite fashion-wise. There was Henry, in his plain beige chino shorts and dark red short-sleeved collared shirt. Nic, meanwhile, sat with his knees together and legs to one side, wearing a flared black skirt and bright pink suspenders.

"Me too." Henry shifted against the sand to find a more comfortable position. He kept his iced coffee close to his chest to avoid spills. "I can't believe it took us so long for our paths to cross."

"Well, Denver isn't exactly next door. Thank you for coming all this way!" Nic gulped his frozen iced Slurpee. "I usually open the meetings talking about some little PSA or whatever the local news is. Lately I've been talking about PrEP a lot. I think these guys are bored of it, but I've found a new victim."

Henry laughed. "Go on," he said, since Nic was clearly so passionate. He'd been pretty quiet up to this point, apart from a little small talk.

"So my boyfriend Kyle works at an HIV charity, Plus. He's taught me a lot, and it's Plus that helps fund this support group so people can afford transit to come to our regular meetings. We have a support group specifically for HIV-positive trans people now." Nic beamed proudly. "I've been helping him a lot, so I've become an advocate for helping trans guys access PrEP and sexual health info. Bridging the gap, so to speak."

"So, uh, I had a question I meant to ask," Will said, frowning. "I started PrEP and I put that on my Grindr profile. I've suddenly got a whole bunch more messages from guys who want to bareback, and I... don't. Is it okay if I just... *don't* tell people I'm on it?"

"Yeah," Nic said, lighting up. "Totally. It's about your health, not their wishlist. Kyle never told me he was on PrEP until we moved in together. It's not that he didn't trust me. It was just none of my business, and part of his everyday routine."

As Will and the other guys asked a couple more questions, Henry stayed silent and absorbed as much as he could.

He'd heard of it in leaflets on the counter of Buckle, but he'd never even thought about it himself. Not that he'd needed it, but he admired the guys who did for talking about it so openly.

He'd avoided trans support groups after the first few months of this journey, because they'd definitely never talked about this kind of stuff. Things had changed a lot in a decade.

It made him feel all warm and fuzzy just seeing the support they showed for each other, and how much Nic clearly cared about them all. Like he was home, at last, among his own people.

Henry's phone went off and he quickly glanced at it, his adrenaline rushing. *Is Jaden in trouble?*

But what he saw was a photo of Jaden sitting next to Cece, looking up into the camera with a grin. That was Jaden's way of letting him know he was okay, and it did Henry's heart good. He grinned at the picture and saved it to his phone, sent a heart emoji back, and pocketed it.

He could focus on this now.

"So, what's the meeting today, boss?" Will spoke up with a cheeky grin.

Nic glanced at Henry. "Usually we have a theme. But I thought we'd keep this one loose and just check in with everyone. No obligation to say anything, of course. But if you want to talk about anything—here's your chance."

"Well, uh..." Henry cleared his throat and smiled at the rest of the guys. "It's really cool to be here. So thank you for inviting me today. I haven't met another out trans guy since... well, since the waiting room at my first hormone clinic. And I wouldn't call that *meeting*, exactly."

"Just the signal," Jake said with a grin and an upnod as the others laughed. "That one."

Henry laughed and nodded. "Yeah. But today's been awesome. I've been in stealth mode for like, five years. And I'm just—literally this week—starting to change that."

Looking around the group, Henry smiled. It made his heart sing in a way he hadn't expected to see such a diverse group. Some of them, like Nic, were in eyeliner and looking super femme. Others, like Jake and Henry himself, wore button-up shirts and shorts.

From twinky, fresh-faced young Will in bright pink lipstick and a tube top to the quiet Patrick in a plaid shirt and ripped jeans, it felt like he was surrounded by *possibilities*.

Henry wasn't unhappy with the way he looked, but he'd just never seen any other options. He'd tried so hard, and for so long, to blend in with the rugged, outdoorsy guys who surrounded him. And even if he didn't want to branch out into winged eyeliner sharp enough to kill a man, it was refreshing to see guys who were so confident in themselves.

Was this what he'd been missing over the last few years? Six trans guys in one place—it made Henry's whole world reel. He'd *never* felt like he was surrounded by his own people, even in gay bars. Even there, he was always on his guard.

But here, there was no need to explain who he was or where he'd come from. No need to bite his tongue and ignore the kick in the gut when the people around him laughed about body parts he'd once had. And sure as hell no need to be nervous.

Even so, his pulse fluttered a little too quickly.

"So, um… things are a little scary. Even here, I feel like maybe someone will *spot me* here and report back to the gender police." He chuckled sheepishly. "I've just started dating this guy and he's super supportive. But I'm coming out at work, too."

"What do you do?" Will asked, pushing his big pop-star sunglasses up his nose.

"Wilderness guide." Henry smiled. "I love it. But it can get pretty... what's the word..." He drew two boxes in the sand with his fingertip.

"Binary?" Nic suggested with a knowing smile.

"That's it." Henry let out a sigh and sipped his coffee again. "I just told my favorite coworker—he's pretty much my best friend. And he'd already guessed. But my boss... I don't know how he'll take it. So... uh... anyone with advice?"

Mack, hiding behind sideswept black hair with dyed blue tips and an emo T-shirt, raised his hand slightly. "I'm pretty much stealth. I'm going to community college, though; that's kind of different."

"No, go on." Henry wanted to take in everything he could today—like he'd been deficient in vitamin T and suddenly it was suffusing him with excitement.

"Well, I tell my doctors and people I date." Mack tossed his head, pushing his hair out of the way. "But I don't even like to do that. I just want to be... any other boy."

Henry nodded slightly. Mack didn't have to explain it; he knew. "I felt like that too, for years. But I don't now. It feels like whatever I was healing inside me... it's done. I don't know. I feel restless, I guess."

Nic hummed. "Well, nobody's obligated to come out. That's like, ground rules 101," he said as everyone in the group nodded. "And nobody's obligated to stay a hundred percent in the closet, either. Some people think we should do that." He waved a hand up and down himself and grinned. "Obviously not me… but I struggled a bit with it."

Henry stirred his coffee with his straw, the ice cubes gently clunking against the sides of the cup. "Yeah?"

"I moved, way far away from my whole family and everything. Threw out everything even remotely girly. Made a fresh start. Then I… I don't know. I got curious. Started buying just a few makeup things, but I was too scared to wear them. Then I met a guy," Nic said with a grin. "Kyle's way more femme than I am. Any day of the week. I stole these," he plucked the suspenders with his thumb, "from his closet. He's helped me get more comfortable in so many ways. But, man—end of the day, we only get one life. Do you, boo. It's scary as shit, but the people who matter will stick around."

As the other guys chimed in with agreement and snippets of their own stories, Henry nodded slowly.

Do me, he thought. *Well, that's not changing. They all know me. It's not like I'm yearning to get more femme like Nic was. I'm just adding a little bit to my background story. Not editing it out.*

Henry caught his breath. "Editing it out," he repeated, but out loud this time. "That's… how it's felt to me. Not like I'm hiding it, but like I'm always watching myself."

"Gender policing. That shit gets internalized," Will said with a sage nod. His boyfriend, a sweet but quiet guy named Caleb, drew little shapes in the sand and nodded.

"Yeah. I just want to let go of *watching* myself all the time. Like it's a pass/fail test," Henry chuckled.

"Ugh, *passing*," Mack muttered. "I mean, I'd say I pass pretty well, but even I hate it."

"Well, I don't." Will's voice was sharp. "And I wish I could, but…"

Henry felt a twist of guilt in his stomach. *I did, up until I decided not to.* He bit his lip. But what sounded like an escape to some of them had become his cage, and there was no way he could explain that.

As a couple of the guys shifted uncomfortably, Nic interjected gently, "We don't compare passability in this group. That's something we can too easily use to hurt ourselves and each other."

Henry cleared his throat. "Sorry. I think I started that one. But I guess I just want to hear that it's okay to stop trying so hard." *Oof,* he thought. As he said it out loud, the tension in his shoulders drained and his chest eased. "Wow. Yeah. It *is* okay."

That was something they could all agree with. Nods and murmurs swept through the group.

"So it's coming out at work you're worried about?" Nic asked.

Henry nodded. "My boss is gay-friendly, but I think that's where he draws the line." The looks of recognition on people's faces made him relax even more. He *wasn't* crazy or imagining it. Accepting one part of the rainbow meant jackshit about whether they'd accept *all* of Henry.

"Is it something where you can find another job easily, or...?" Nic trailed off.

Henry nodded. "I've actually wanted to start my own outfit for a while. So I stuck with this one cause their health insurance was pretty good for surgeries. Well, I'm all done with those... I've got the co-pay loans to pay off, but I'm nearly there."

"That's awesome." Jake practically sparkled as he grinned at him. "Congrats."

"Thanks." Henry tried to brush it off, not wanting anyone

else to feel that deep-rooted envy he'd once felt reading people's stories online—the gut-twisting, sleepless nights he didn't miss one tiny bit. "But yeah, I've wanted to start a regular event for taking trans people hiking or camping or something. Like a trans summer camp."

He nearly fell backward in the sand at the excitement that was met with.

"Trans summer camp!" Will took off his sunglasses and gestured with them. "*Hell yes*. Dude, you have no idea how much I wanna swim around people who won't stare at my chest."

There were nods and emphatic sounds of agreement. "And like, learn to do stuff outdoors," said Mack.

"Have someone to hike with who gets *why* I'm winded and stops with me when I need it," Pat said.

Jake interjected, "Bathroom. Breaks."

"Oh my God, yes."

Henry's head whirled as he grabbed his phone, typing in notes as quickly as he could. And it wasn't just his head, either. His heart felt like it was cracking wide open like it hadn't in a very long time.

He almost took for granted now that he felt *right*. Gender dysphoria had given way to gender euphoria. But a few months after each surgery, the exhilarating high had settled and left him wondering what was next.

Without crushing dysphoria keeping him moving and looking for escapes, Henry's life had settled into something static and... well, not quite right for him anymore. He'd been stuck in this place, trying to figure out what was next.

Until now.

Now, he had an idea. And it was scary, and he was pretty sure Jaden would call him crazy, but it made him feel *right* again. The only question was how on earth he'd make it work—especially if Damien reacted like Henry was expecting him to.

But Henry's dream had come true when he'd found Jaden. All his dreams felt within reach.

CHAPTER
Eighteen
JADEN

WAKING UP PRESSED AGAINST HENRY FILLED JADEN WITH happiness from his head to the tips of his toes. Or maybe that was his *other* head, which was pressed between Henry's thighs. His morning wood throbbed in a steady pulse of need that quickly banished all thoughts of sleeping in.

Jaden was spooning him now—or trying to, at least. It felt like he was a stuffed animal clinging to Henry's back and trying to hug a tree. He grinned to himself, stretching and pushing closer.

Every nerve in his cock sparked to life as his sensitive skin brushed the furry, warm thighs that were pressed so perfectly together.

"Mmph," Henry mumbled quietly, sighing as he stretched to life. Then he paused and chuckled, his voice deep and catching. "What's this?" One hand ran down the mattress, under the sheets, and suddenly sensation exploded across the head of Jaden's cock. A fingertip traced around the head, just where it poked out from the gap of Henry's thighs, resting against his balls.

"My gift to you," Jaden giggled softly. "Or maybe your gift to me. If I fucked your thighs like this, could I get you hard?"

"You'd have to ram into my balls pretty hard," Henry mumbled with a sleepy chuckle. "I don't think that'd be a positive experience for either of us."

"Damn it. I'll have to do it the manual way." Jaden moved quickly, slipping his hand over Henry and groping his way to his cock.

Henry gasped and laughed, trying to smack away Jaden's hand. Within moments, they were tussling under the covers, and Jaden had no complaints. He spent more time grinding against Henry, moaning softly at the thrill of his cock against bare, hot skin, than actually trying to win—whatever winning was supposed to be right now.

"I know how to solve this," Jaden finally panted when they were done wrestling, the covers kicked to the bottom of the bed, his head in the crook of Henry's arm, face smushed against his chest.

"How's that?" Henry asked.

In answer, Jaden just licked Henry's nipple. *No, wait, damn it.* He still forgot sometimes that that wouldn't have the effect it might were the situation reversed.

So he squirmed free and spun around until he faced away from Henry, straddling his stomach.

"Yeehaw, cowboy," Henry teased and smacked his ass.

Jaden gasped and dissolved into giggles again, but he was on a mission. A very important mission that involved dicks and a certain number.

"Ohhh," Henry gasped as Jaden shifted onto all fours. "I like the way you think."

Jaden grinned at his view of that delicious cock and balls, ready for the taking. Henry's lips brushed against Jaden's hard-on, and he whimpered. While Henry kissed his length from base to tip, making tremors of pleasure shake their way through Jaden's whole body, he tried his best to focus on not sucking at this exchange—by sucking.

Jaden wrapped his hand around the base of Henry's dick, squeezing firmly, as he knew Henry liked.

Henry's hot, wet mouth slid around his shaft, his tongue teasing at Jaden's already-wet slit. *Fuck, that's good,* Jaden thought, but he couldn't spare a moment for speech. Instead, he wrapped his lips around the head of that thick, still-soft cock and sucked it firmly into his mouth with a loud, wet sound.

"Mmm!" Henry's noise was muffled, but it vibrated straight through Jaden's shaft into the deep of his belly. His thighs trembled again, and he shifted his forearm to stay braced above Henry. It was all he could do not to fuck Henry's gorgeous mouth.

Especially since Henry seemed to be tempting him to, drawing his tongue in broad, slow motions up and down the shaft.

As Jaden whimpered and squirmed, he sucked hard, flicking his tongue around the head until he heard Henry gasp. Then he slid his mouth down, taking in as much of Henry's cock as he could without choking.

His other hand wandered up Henry's thigh, and then he gently traced his fingers around Henry's balls until he found that little switch under the skin.

He pressed firmly, whimpering with pleasure as Henry's cock responded to his touch by growing harder in his mouth. Slowly he repeated this rhythm, bobbing his head down and pumping Henry up, just a little at a time.

Henry's soft cock swelling to life in his mouth was the most addictive mouthfeel Jaden had ever known.

"Mmmph," Henry moaned, throaty and deep, the noise clearly approving. His nails dug into Jaden's hips as he deep-throated him until the head of Jaden's cock bumped the ridges of Henry's throat.

Best of all, Henry brushed one finger down Jaden's spine —and then kept going, tracing between his cheeks all the way to his tight little hole.

Oh, Jesus, that's incredible!

Jaden's moan was quick and high, his head spinning as electric jolts flipped his stomach inside-out and crackled through him. Blood rushed south, stiffening his cock even further.

He wasn't entirely sure he *wouldn't* just blow his load in Henry's mouth on the spot.

Jaden pulled his mouth off Henry and gasped for breath. "Baby, I can't—that's too good," he whimpered. "I won't last long."

He couldn't help it—he thrust in short, sharp jerks, enjoying every damn second of his cock in and out of the swollen, beautiful lips. Jaden wanted to wake up every day to Henry's wet mouth around him, his strong grip on his hips as his tongue danced around his cock.

"Mmhmm," Henry managed around his cock. He pulled Jaden into him by the hips and then rolled them over carefully, until he hovered above him.

Jaden loved that feeling of being blanketed by him. He squirmed against the bed and whimpered in pleasure. The muffled grunts and moans of encouragement drove Jaden onward, so he kept kissing the tip of Henry's shaft.

He adored the soft, uniquely fuzzy outer layer of Henry's

cock. Jaden focused on licking the head so he could squeeze the base and jerk him in slow motions. His fist touched his lips and then slid back down—up, really, since he was under him—to the base of Henry's cock.

Before long, he had the rhythm down pat, but Henry won as usual by utterly distracting him. Henry wrapped his hand around the base of Jaden's shaft and let the other tease between Jaden's thighs, walking his way past his balls to his hole once again.

Jaden's cry was swift and loud as he threw his head back into the mattress, his feet touching the wall. He spread his legs instantly, bending his knees so Henry could finger him if he wanted to.

"Yes," Jaden panted while Henry ground against his lips, that hard cock filling his line of sight. "Baby, yes." He squeezed Henry and jerked him off hard and fast, sucking just the tip of his cock.

All the while, Henry was drawing slow circles around his quivering hole, lighting up nerves Jaden had almost forgotten about.

Jesus, how much he wanted Henry inside him right now. He wanted to be stretched wide open and filled to the hilt, bent in two as Henry fucked him into the mattress.

Fuck. There was no stopping it. Jaden gasped and choked on Henry's cock as Henry pushed into his mouth while pushing just the tip of one wet finger inside him.

Visions of Henry fucking him hard and fast, then sweet and tender, danced through Jaden's head. He wanted to be sitting on Henry's lap, riding him. He wanted Henry to pin him against the wall. He wanted to bend over the bed and grab the edge while Henry slammed into him.

"Mm—" Jaden grunted as pleasure exploded in his brain

and through every nerve ending in his body. His voice was muffled by Henry's thick arousal fucking his mouth while he sucked Jaden's cock and teased him with a finger, too.

Jaden's world narrowed to just the pulsing of his cock, the pounding of his heart, and every inch of the hot, rippling, muscled body that hovered over him.

Pleasure came from all directions, and with one more stifled cry, Jaden was lost to it. The wave hit him sharp and fast, blacking out everything else. Henry finally shifted up onto all fours and slid out of his mouth.

Jaden crashed over the edge and squeezed his eyes shut, bucking off the bed and pushing into Henry's mouth. And then he realized Henry was swallowing, sucking every drop of Jaden's hot, wet load as it hit his tongue.

"Yes," Jaden whimpered softly, gripping Henry's thighs. His head was still spinning, every inch of his body suddenly draining of the tension he'd hardly noticed gripping him. "Your turn."

Henry growled and rolled off Jaden, quickly turning around so he could straddle Jaden's chest and sit upright above him. He locked eyes with Jaden and reached down to cup his cheek with one hand.

"Watch me," Henry breathed out.

How the hell could Jaden ever want to do anything else? Fuck, Henry was the most gorgeous man Jaden had ever seen. His eyes were fierce and dark, his hand wrapped around the base of his shaft as he jerked off hard and fast.

"Yes," Jaden whimpered, his gaze locked on that thick length above him. And Henry's face was beautiful right now, his lips pressed tightly together as his nose scrunched up and his breathing came in heavy, quick pants.

He was so close he had to be ready to burst.

"Come for me, baby," Jaden gasped. "Your turn."

"I'm—I can't stop," Henry managed, his breathing ragged. He swayed forward and grabbed the headboard above Jaden, his stroking slowing just a fraction as his eyes widened.

Jaden knew what that meant. He instinctively narrowed his eyes against stray droplets for a moment, only to remember he didn't have to worry about that. He could look all he wanted.

And that he did, grinning up at him. "Yes, Henry…!" He was going to be daydreaming about *this* moment all day long.

"I…" Henry trailed off, his lips moved silently. *Yes*, he seemed to be mouthing, his lips widening into an O shape before he threw his head back and cried out once, sharply.

Jaden stared running his hands up the backs of Henry's thighs to squeeze his ass gently. Muscles rippled under him, and Henry's hips jerked forward as he thrust into the tight ring of his fingers. The sharp, erratic movements gradually slowed as Henry gasped for breath.

Finally he rolled his head forward again to meet Jaden's look with glazed eyes and a loopy grin. "Oh, man."

"Oh, *man*," Jaden agreed in awe, running his hands up Henry's sides now. "Come here so I can kiss you."

"Mmm. Yeah." Henry scooted down the bed swiftly, but he was still limp as he hit the bed on his side next to Jaden.

Jaden giggled and cuddled into him, pressing kisses against his jaw. "Oh, fuck, that was hot. I hope you liked waking up that way."

"Yeah… I… *yeah*." Henry shook his head as if trying to put together coherent words.

"Yeah?" Jaden teased, kissing Henry until he stopped smiling enough that he could suck his lower lip between his teeth.

Henry pulled back from the kiss to catch his breath, shaking his head. "Yeah," he mumbled again, making Jaden burst into giggles.

Then Cece whined and they both looked over to the other bed where she'd decided to sleep. She was awake now, lying on her back with her tail thumping gently like she hoped to look extra-adorable and get extra breakfast.

Henry laughed and then caught his breath as he looked over at the bedside table. "Ah, shit. It's getting late, and we have a long drive ahead of us."

Jaden pouted. "Yeah. You're right." He didn't want this trip to end—which was a far cry from how he'd thought he'd feel about it.

Last night had been perfect. After meeting up, they'd walked hand-in-hand to get ice cream and talk about their afternoons. That alone had been a big step forward for them.

They were so proud of each other—Henry proud of Jaden for visiting that spot and coming to realize it didn't hold power over him anymore; Jaden proud of Henry for meeting other trans people and deciding to come out and be proud instead of letting his fear rule him.

"Gotta go back to boring real life and work and shit," Jaden sighed.

Henry pressed a kiss on his lips. "Maybe so. But we have a whole hell of a lot left to explore together."

And that was a promise that made Jaden's whole body sing in all the best ways.

They'd confronted their fears and grown so much in these past few weeks. They were over the hardest parts—and they'd done it together. Nothing could stop them now.

CHAPTER
Nineteen

JADEN

AFTER NIGHTS OF CRAPPY MOTEL PILLOWS AND MATTRESSES, simply waking up in his own bed was delightful.

The drive home had been long as hell. Henry was a trooper, never complaining about it, but when he'd left Jaden's house, it felt…

Well, it felt quiet. Too quiet. Smaller, colder, and lonelier.

It was barely a few minutes before seven. Almost time to start his shift. After years of rolling out of bed to his desk, Jaden hardly remembered commuting at all. He'd barely have time for breakfast before he started, but that was okay.

He only really came to his senses after he'd made himself coffee and fed Cece. He'd walk her on his first break. Jaden scarfed his bagel as fast as he could, keeping an eye on the clock. As long as he logged on in the next couple of minutes, he'd be fine.

He was barely dressed before there was a knock on the door.

Wait, is that… Henry? Spence was never up this early. But it was first thing in the morning, and Henry was supposed to be up anyway—on his way to another day trip. Maybe it had been cancelled.

Jaden scrambled to his feet with a grin and headed for the door, already thinking up ways to not show up for his shift. Could he call in sick? His bosses wouldn't mind; Jaden *never* took time off work.

But when he opened it, it wasn't Henry at all.

It was that asshole Ron, the property manager. He was sneering at Jaden again, like he always did. "The dog's yours, isn't it?" was his greeting, like he'd won some game Jaden hadn't even known they were playing.

"Uh…" Still half-asleep and groggy, Jaden didn't have anything to say to that.

"I thought as much. Dogs aren't allowed in the building. You'll have to get rid of her, or send her to live with your…" Ron trailed off meaningfully, raising an eyebrow.

Whoa. Wait. Not cool. That made Jaden jolt to life, his back stiffening. "What? No, sir," he responded, trying not to grit his teeth. "She's an emotional support animal, not a pet."

"I don't care if she's a circus pony." Ron waved off his attempt to interrupt and keep explaining. "We can't have pet hair in the building, and that's just that."

Jaden had done his homework beforehand. Cece had sensed his distress and come over, and she was leaning on his leg now to ground him. Jaden put a hand on her head instinctively and drew himself up. "No, I know what the law says."

"Look, kid." Ron sighed and scratched his jaw, rolling his head back like he'd rather be doing anything else. "You got a choice. Your better option is to quietly leave at the end of the month. I'll even put in a word about your damage deposit." He glanced over Jaden's shoulder like he expected to see Cece-shaped holes in the walls or something.

Jaden's whole body went stiff with fear as Cece leaned into him even harder. He couldn't think of anything else he could do or say to this guy, when he'd so clearly made up his mind.

So he shut the door in Ron's face.

"Shit," Jaden whispered after a few moments of staring at the now-closed door in stunned silence.

Cece tailed him to the living room, and as soon as Jaden sat, she draped her weight across his lap.

Okay. That helped. A little bit, anyway.

What the hell was Jaden going to do? Should he fight back? How much would that cost? God, then he'd have to go *out* to a courthouse or something.

The more he thought about the idea, the more he hated it.

But however hard Jaden tried to think about it, he couldn't come up with an answer. He called in sick to work, and as he'd thought, his manager was cool with it.

God, how he wished he had a better reason for pulling a sickie than trying to figure out how to stop his life from falling apart just as it seemed to fit together.

Jaden finally recovered his wits and texted Henry. He had no idea what exactly to say, so he dithered about it for a few minutes before finally settling on something neutral. He'd wait to drop the bombshell until they were in person. That was better, right?

Loved this morning <3 Free tonight?

Henry's response was surprisingly fast—and terse.

Can't come today babe. Raincheck?

Jaden stared at the message for a good few minutes, trying to sort out his feelings. Was Henry mad at him? Was he tired of him? Was he second-guessing their relationship now that they were back home from the road trip?

And why, even though he knew better, was Jaden even entertaining these thoughts?

Finally, it clicked. This was how Jaden's asshole ex had cut things off. Even though he logically knew better, some small part of him was convinced that this meant it was over with Henry.

And this *was* a weirdly terse message for Henry. If Jaden hadn't wanted to push and tell him the reason before, he especially didn't want to now.

"Oh, Jesus," Jaden muttered, burying his face in Cece's fur and hugging her to him. "Well, one thing's for sure. You're staying, which means I'm going. Somehow."

He didn't want to call Spence for help and undermine all the things he'd promised his brother just days ago about relying on him less. But he also couldn't see a choice right now. Moving day—on his own—was a thought he couldn't even process.

What the hell was he going to do?

CHAPTER

Twenty

HENRY

H ENRY WAS FINALLY GOING TO GET A READ ON D AMIEN. T HE two of them were working together. With nobody else around this morning before the busload of summer camp kids arrived, it was the perfect chance.

Maybe he wouldn't come out to him—maybe he never would. But he could at least suggest the trans camping idea as a spinoff of his gay hiking groups, and feel things out.

If Damien shut it down, Henry would know for his own sake that it wasn't safe to come out. If not, he could decide if he wanted to take that risk.

Henry could steer a kayak down a whitewater current or build a fire from scratch after nightfall. This ought to be easy. Right?

But his good mood was punctured by confusion the moment he walked into the cabin. Damien knelt there on the floor with Ryan, sorting through lifejackets.

What was Ryan doing here? As far as Henry knew, this was the only trip today.

"Hey," Henry greeted Damien.

"Oh... hey?" Damien greeted, glancing up at him impassively and then back to the life jackets. "What's up?"

"I'm here to... work?" Henry offered uncertainly. For a moment he kicked himself, noticing that his voice had risen like he was trying to be polite on the phone. *But then I'm trying not to give a shit about that,* he reminded himself, so he brushed it off.

"What? With the camp kids? No, man. I had Ryan down to work with me." Damien tossed one of the lifejackets with busted straps to Ryan, who put it on a pile.

Once he'd done so, Ryan raised a hand and waved... but he didn't look up and meet Henry's eyes. His gaze stayed glued to what he was doing.

Neither of them were acting right. It didn't take a genius to work out what was going on.

Motherfucker, Henry thought. He folded his arms and shook his head. "No, man. I told you before I left, see you Monday."

"Did you?" Damien frowned. "Sorry. I must have missed that. It's definitely Ryan's day to work today. You can check the schedule in the office."

The implication he left hanging was, *And you're not trying to steal his trips, are you?*

Henry didn't want to even bother, but he took and released a deep breath. He had a one-night kayaking trip with a few families, and then a bigger group of kids next weekend, too.

Or, he'd *had.*

When Henry walked past the two of them and into the office, he knew what he'd see before his eyes even landed on the paper schedule thumbtacked to the wall.

His week was clear. And that was a *lot* of hours to miss out on.

Henry stepped out of the office, forcing himself to keep his arms unfolded and his tone from growing hostile. "I know what's going on. Why don't you want me on any of those trips?"

"Oh, uh." Damien swiped a hand over his forehead and shrugged, rising to his feet. "Some of the parents would object, you know. No hard feelings. It's just better to keep you to the... other trips. I'll text you if anything comes up this week, okay?"

What the hell? Henry's blood boiled, but he had to pretend he didn't know damn well what they both knew. This wasn't about his sexuality at all.

"No. I can work with the kids. You've never let homo-phobes win before," Henry said flatly. "Is there a problem now?"

He wanted to force Damien to admit it. Not that it would ever stand up in court if Damien made up some bullshit excuse that he'd never actually had Henry down for those shifts at all.

Damien let out a long sigh and shook his head. "It's not just that, and you know it. *Henry*," he said.

A chill ran down Henry's spine. He knew what was going on. It was the air-quote voice.

That was the tone people used when they wanted Henry to know they'd happily call him *it*, and hid behind saying the right name so that he couldn't technically object.

Like the kids in his old school years ago, Damien suddenly thought he knew Henry better than Henry knew himself. For the first time, he said Henry's name like it was a special favor that he didn't deserve and should be grateful for. It was enough to send a sickening wave of nausea through him.

Damien knew perfectly well that he held this power, and he was trying to exploit it. Trying to wake up Henry's worst demons again. He *wanted* Henry to feel less than human.

No, worse still. People fell over correcting themselves if they used the wrong name or gender for Cece. But apparently a trans person didn't warrant that much human decency.

And all of that was packed into a tiny shift in his tone.

"What, then?" Henry's voice was tight. He was done pretending to be polite.

Ryan hummed the national anthem, loud and awkward, and strode out of the cabin with an armful of lifejackets. The total lack of subtlety would have been hilarious in any other situation, but now it just underscored the thick tension in the room with nobody else there.

No witnesses, either, Henry's brain reminded him.

"You lied to me," Damien said quietly, shaking his head.

Henry scoffed. "I've sure as hell never lied to you in my life. My personal life is my own damn business and nobody else's. Now, you never let my being gay hold me back before. Which is how I've become one of your best guides."

Damien paused for a moment, his jaw tight. He conceded that with a slight nod. "You are. That's what's so disappointing. I don't know what trips I'll put you on now. I'll have to think about it."

"No." Henry forced himself to grit the word out. "No, that's not good enough."

Damien spread his hands, then bent to grab the other lifejackets, hooking his fingers through as many straps as possible. "Dunno what else to do. Head home. I'll call you."

"No, you really won't. At least have the decency to tell the truth," Henry told him quietly. "I always have. I'm every inch the man you thought you knew."

Damien's flat stare in return told Henry all he needed to know. This working relationship was over.

He turned and strode on his heel to the car, barely waiting until it was on before throwing it into reverse.

Henry barely remembered the drive. He was shaken to the core, yet too numb to work out what he should do about it.

Even unlocking the front door of his house was a monumental task. His hands shook so badly he dropped his keys.

"Fuck," Henry hissed, resting his palms and forehead against the door. "Fuck, fuck, fuck."

The world hadn't allowed Henry to be soft or delicate in the early years of his journey. Exactly when he'd been most vulnerable, he'd had to defend himself—against his teachers and classmates, against doctors and friends, and against potential lovers.

The fierce anger he'd been forced to develop as a shield still lay close under his skin. It had come back when he most needed it. But now that he was alone, it melted away and all that was left was the ugly, raw devastation he hadn't tasted in years.

Henry didn't want to make a scene on his front porch and get the neighbors involved. So he took several deep breaths and finally bent over, scooping up the keyring and unlocking the door before he could lose his focus.

As soon as he was inside, he called Trip. All he needed to know was whether Damien had shared this little plan with Trip. Trip would have given him a heads up if he'd known—unless he hadn't wanted to disturb Henry on vacation.

His best friend answered after one ring. "Hey man, what's up?"

Okay. Thank God. From his tone, Trip had clearly had no idea what was coming.

"Um… it's bad," Henry murmured. "He heard. Damien. He must have overheard us. Uh, he's wiped me from the schedule for the week. We had a talk, and… he said I've lied to him, and I think he's pretty much…" He almost tripped over his words, still hardly able to believe it. "Basically… He's, uh. He's trying to fire me."

"*Douchebag*," Trip spat out. "Fucking scummy *rat*. I'm on my way over right now. Was I on the schedule?"

"Y-Yeah?" Henry could still picture it clearly—his row had been the only blank one on the schedule. Why would Damien fire him, too?

Trip cursed. "Not anymore. I'm not working a day for him unless you are. I'm on my way over."

Henry's jaw dropped. Trip would do *that* for him, in solidarity? "Man," was all he came up with. "O—Okay."

When his phone went off a moment later, it took Henry a few moments to even process the text. It was from Jaden.

Loved this morning <3 Free tonight?

Oh, Jesus. It was a close call for a few moments whether Henry wanted to laugh or cry.

The very last thing he was capable of right now was feeling sexy, even for Jaden. Henry would be a hot mess if he took him up on that offer.

Talking this through on the phone wouldn't work, either. He needed to have an answer. Without that, he'd be lost. He couldn't be the strong, sexy man Jaden expected. No, that he *wanted* Jaden to see. Just a scared little boy again, the way he hadn't felt for years.

Jaden had been so pleased and proud of him for coming out. What would he think now? Would Jaden worry what it would mean for their life together? *Would* Henry be a burden on him?

What would Jaden's parents think? Or Spence?

Poor Jaden was scared about people's reactions to them as a gay couple. What if Henry being trans would always bring him even more trouble?

What if this was just the beginning?

Henry typed out the only response he could think of.

Can't come today babe. Raincheck?

He almost giggled through the wave of nausea that swamped him. He couldn't come in any of the ways Jaden probably wanted from him. And boy, did that thought hurt.

Henry wanted to be sick. He slumped down the wall, pressing his phone into his head. He hadn't even taken his shoes off. Didn't think he could stand up straight. No, definitely couldn't. The floor was the best place right now.

That last thought kept echoing around his head, drumming into him the notes of fear.

What if this is just the beginning?

Now that he was being open about this, Henry didn't want to go back in that closet. He'd *just* gotten his first taste of life, unfiltered. Of real freedom.

He'd lived in too many fucking closets in his life to ever be able to do it again. He just couldn't. But that left the future even wider open with terrifying possibilities.

Henry had no idea what percentage of people in his life were going to be dicks about it. Right now he was at a 1-in-3 ratio, and that… that wasn't good.

No, I came out to the guys on the trip, too. 1-in-7. Right? But they're not people I see every day. Does that count? Henry thought, rubbing his head.

Logically, he knew his online trans friends would all say it wasn't his fault. That Damien was a bigoted asshole that he shouldn't want to work for anyway. He could find a better job with someone who had his head screwed on straight. It was the perfect chance. He even knew they'd be right to say it.

But it didn't *feel* that way, when Henry had been getting along fine for years. Only now—after finally working up the courage to show a bit of himself he could persuade himself that he hadn't even *needed* to...

Now everything had changed.

Thank God Trip banged on the door, and then pushed it open. "Dude? Your keys are still in the door—ah, Christ." He saw Henry on the floor and groaned, crouching next to him. "Henry, man. I'm sorry."

"No. I'm sorry," Henry muttered, swiping at his eyes with embarrassment. His throat was tight and choked up.

Trip grabbed him around the shoulders and squeezed the life out of him, which at least brought a momentary smile to Henry's face. He'd been telling the truth—he wasn't treating him an ounce differently.

Good. There was some normalcy in Henry's world right now.

"It's time," Trip said, pulling back at last and offering Henry a hand to his feet.

Henry took it and stood, wobbly but a little less nauseated by the idea of ever facing the world again. "Time...?"

"To start our own outfit. You and me. We have more than enough experience between us. We can split the licensing costs and stuff. He wants you to feel like you're under his thumb, and you're not. You could have walked away two years ago, and he'd run the place into the dust without you."

A blush crept over Henry's cheeks. Sure, he'd helped out with this and that—okay, maybe everything. But it had all seemed like part of the job. Like a little family business. There was just one thing.

"But he doesn't have a problem with you," Henry said, frowning slightly. "Are you sure?"

Trip scoffed. "You don't get to turn down my help, man," he said sternly. He steered Henry to the dining room table and sat him down, pulling out a chair and turning it backward to sit beside him.

But he's giving up his job just because of me. Henry opened and shut his mouth a few times, trying to think of a way to talk him out of it.

Trip grinned. "I've been looking for a reason to get clear of that prick for years. Yeah, he pretended to be cool about the gay thing. But that was just cause it brought in money, *using* you as a gay guy, and he doesn't think he can use you the same way because of your… you know, historical gender or whatever."

Wow. Trip had a point there. Henry shut his mouth in a hurry as that sank in, and his gut didn't tell him otherwise.

"Historical gender," was the only thing Henry could think to repeat, another chuckle slipping free.

"Did I say that wrong?" Trip's forehead creased with concern.

Henry's laughter only grew as he shook his head. "Yeah, but it's all right. Historical gender just sounds like a long-buried artifact for archaeologists to dig up."

Trip grinned and clapped his shoulder. "There's Henry again. You're nuts," he said fondly. "Coffee?"

Henry banged his forehead on the dining room table. "Please."

"It's not quite drinks at Buckle like I wanted," Trip called out from the kitchen as he rattled around in the mug cupboard. "But before I leave today, this plan is coming together. We'll get the ball rolling on permits. And *then* we can go out and drink to you being way too good for that asshole. Now go search for the small business department. We're gonna need to make some calls."

A sigh of relief escaped Henry as he tugged his laptop toward him and opened it.

Yeah. Trip was right. He could handle this. With his best friend by his side, it would be even easier. They'd talked for years about doing it.

And tomorrow, when he'd figured out how not to feel like a ticking time bomb bringing trouble to Jaden's life, Henry would break the news to him.

But first, one thing at a time.

JADEN HAD AN IDEA. BY ALL RIGHTS, IT WAS A BATSHIT IDEA, but it sank its claws into him.

He needed to talk to Henry—today. And Jaden had the sneaking suspicion that something was up with Henry.

Jaden didn't want to stay at home and make Henry come to him. It was no longer a safe place—nor even a golden cage, offering safety at the price of clipped wings. Instead, it had suddenly morphed.

Jaden didn't feel safe there. Not with Ron breathing down his neck whenever he so much as checked the mailbox, sneering at Cece, mysteriously standing in the lobby glaring at them every time they walked through it.

He had no doubt that moving out would be easier than staying and fighting the property manager, who could try to make his life hell in plenty of little ways. But there were no nice, easy solutions.

He also didn't want to meet Henry at his own house, because even though he had the address, this conversation… couldn't happen on his territory. The last thing he wanted was Henry to feel like he was forced into offering Jaden his home or time.

No, it needed to be neutral ground. Which meant one thing: the great outdoors.

And *that* brought him to the idea. Things were different. Jaden had Cece, and he'd managed to conquer his own fear of the very worst spot in the world. What could one little trail do to him now?

So he grabbed his phone and sent Henry a text.

I need to talk to you <3

Then Jaden sank onto the floor and put the phone on his coffee table, staring intently at the screen, twisting his hands together.

Cece came to lie next to him and put her chin on his knee.

"Thanks, Cece," Jaden murmured, stroking her gently. The dots that meant Henry was typing back appeared, and he caught his breath.

That was quick. Henry probably wasn't at work, then.

Are you OK? Should I come over? I have some stuff to talk about too. :) I can bring Chinese?

Well, that laid to rest a bunch of Jaden's worries all at once. Henry just had something on his mind. It wasn't like he was going to dump Jaden and run.

No, I want to try a hike. Cece and I will drive up and meet you at the same trail as before.

The response came in almost instantly.

OK, can't wait! See you there <3

The heart at the end made Jaden smile. He sent one back and took a deep breath. "Okay, Cece. Let's do this."

It was, in fact, a terrible idea.

But as the road wound up toward the mountains and the city fell away behind him, Jaden found himself strangely eager. They'd only made it out of the car last time. Anything further would be an improvement.

Jaden had already worked out that this decision was based on mindless panic and the fumes of last night's sleep. Without even a safe home to retreat to, Jaden was losing it a little bit—halfway to Panicville again.

But hey, flying off the handle had gotten him a boyfriend last time.

And this would give him a chance to talk to Henry—to show him how much he was growing. So that way, maybe it wouldn't totally scare him off when he also told him what this change had cost him.

And, most importantly, asked for help.

It didn't have to be sharing his home. Jaden just *wanted* that to be the answer. He wanted with all his heart to be around Henry every minute of every day.

"Okay, girl. Oh, that's his car. Let's park next to him," Jaden said, and he heard the swish and thump of Cece's tail against the backseat in answer.

Once he'd parked, Jaden shut off the car and did his usual trick—distracting himself with Cece.

"Wait," Jaden told Cece, just in case she got excited and forgot her training. Then he climbed out and headed around to her side of the backseat, opening the door and leaning in to unclip her. He clipped her leash onto the vest and stood back, waiting to see what she'd do.

Good. She didn't move, her ears alert and head cocked slightly as she stayed lying on the backseat.

A flicker of pride lit up Jaden's chest. "Unload," he told

her, smiling and stepping aside so she could jump down. Then he shut the door and looked up.

Henry was there, wearing plain cargo shorts and a blue t-shirt with seams along the shoulders. And he looked rougher than Jaden had ever seen him.

"Hi," Henry said with a tired little smile. He opened his arms in an invitation.

"Henry," Jaden breathed out.

Before he even knew it, he was snuggling into Henry's chest, his face pressed into his shoulder while Henry squeezed him with those strong arms like he could pull the pieces of Jaden's life back together.

Even the smell of him and the feel of his warm lips brushing against Jaden's forehead... it made Jaden feel *complete*.

Wait. What?

He'd never believed in the idea of two people being halves that made a whole. Everyone should be a strong and independent person, right? Even if Henry made every little thing about Jaden's life better, sometimes without even trying...

Ah, fuck. Jaden pushed aside *that* thought for later. One thing at a time.

"Shall we? While I've got my courage up?" Jaden asked. He lowered his voice and giggled. "And before you get anything else up?"

"Oh!" Henry pretended to be shocked, that playful little smile returning to his lips. "You naughty little minx."

They set off across the parking lot toward the trailhead, while Jaden tried determinedly to focus on his little family flanking him—Cece on one side, Henry on the other.

Just a few words, and Jaden already felt like a different person. How on earth could he go and find another new place to live and resign himself to these little snatches of time he grabbed with Henry?

"Can we move in together?"

Henry stopped dead and turned to Jaden, his jaw dropping. "Did I... did you...?"

Oh, shit. Jaden wasn't supposed to say *that*. In fact, that was basically the only thing he hadn't wanted to say. But all his worries about not being a burden on Henry, or not rushing into anything in their relationship, had melted away when he was faced with this inescapable truth.

Henry was like the first flush of color in his black-and-white life. Blue, of course. Like the open skies above them, and the crystal-clear orbs of his eyes. All he wanted now was to embrace that color and let it light up his world.

To slip out of his own world and into Henry's—forever.

"Oh, wow," Henry said, a grin stretching across his face. "Where did *that* come from? The road trip was that great, huh?"

Jaden laughed sheepishly. "I—oh, God. My mouth did a thing without permission," Jaden mumbled, covering his face with one hand while gripping Cece's leash with the other. "I didn't mean to lead with that. But I'm serious about you. And I want to show you that I'm serious. And I have to move out soon, and I... oh my God, why can't I put these words together?"

"Phew," Henry breathed out. "Breathe, Jaden. You're pushing yourself a lot right now. Let's just walk for a minute, huh? Tell me any time you want to stop."

So Jaden took his time, slowly walking with Henry, staring down at the trail. Maybe that was the key: keep watching his own feet, or Cece, or Henry. Nothing else.

His head still spun and his words still didn't want to come

out right, but putting one foot in front of the other helped. Vaguely aware they were walking up a gradual hill, he switched off everything else and just… *existed*.

"Okay," Jaden finally murmured when they reached the top. He drew to a halt, letting go of Henry's hand so he could rub his palms dry on his shorts. A quick glance back at the parking lot showed they'd only covered a couple hundred feet.

Damn it. It had felt like a mile.

Yet it felt like Jaden's brain had unclenched, his chest a little less tight.

"Okay?" Henry echoed, stopping in front of him and stepping close. "There's a bench right here. Let's sit."

"Oh, good." Jaden's laugh of relief was shakier than he'd meant it to be. "Perfect. Sit, Cece. Lie down. Wait."

Henry sat on the bench and drew Jaden down next to him. He took both his hands, squeezing lightly. "Okay. You're doing amazing. I didn't expect you to do this today, so soon after the trip. Are you okay?"

Jaden slid close, until he was pressed against Henry's side with Henry's arm around his shoulder. "Not sure what okay is anymore," he murmured.

What the hell had he been thinking? They could have met for a drive or anything—literally anything else. But no, Jaden had gotten cocky. Wanted to prove himself, all over again.

One of these days, Henry would get sick and tired of it.

But he didn't. Instead, Henry just opened his arm in an invitation to slide even closer. "Come here," he murmured. "Nobody else is around. I'll keep an eye out."

Jaden let out a sigh of relief and turned his head to rest his forehead on Henry's shoulder. With Henry shielding him from view of the parking lot, his arm sheltering him from the whole damn world out there, he could focus.

"So, um. Moving in." Jaden licked his lips. "Basically, my landlord found out about Cece, and they don't care about the law, they're treating her like a pet. I don't want to fight them over it."

Henry hissed quietly, his grip on Jaden tightening. "Fuckers," he muttered darkly. "Why didn't you tell me? Your text just sounded like you wanted to hang out! I don't want you to feel like you can't come to me."

"I…" Jaden trailed off, his mouth going dry. "I didn't want you to think I was just using you because I'm too weak to deal with my own life decisions."

Henry stared at him. "What? Babe, no. I… I think you're one of the strongest people I know. You've worked so fucking hard on yourself these last few years, before I even met you."

Jaden groaned. "But I was still… so afraid. So when you texted back, I didn't want to push it. I even thought maybe you were just trying to pull back from me."

"Never." Henry's voice was strong and decisive. "I never would, Jaden. You have to trust me on that. When I'm wrapped up in my own head, it's not your fault."

Jaden let out a deep breath and rested his forehead on Henry's shoulder. "So, I was going to ask you for help finding a new place and moving in, and then I just…"

No, don't tell him. Not yet. It's too soon, isn't it? Jaden thought, but there was no stopping the truth.

"I love being around you. I'm tired of being lonely and… alone. When you're around, it's like everything sparkles. And then you leave and my four walls close in around me, and they're *gray.*" Jaden's frustration poured out as his eyes heated up with unshed tears. "I—I want you around, all the time. I don't want to move to yet another little place on my own and wait for you to come back from trips and get whatever nights I can with you…"

Henry tensed up under Jaden—suddenly, the soft curve of his shoulder went hard as a board.

"Ah. Um…" Henry mumbled.

Jaden's stomach dropped. *Shit. He doesn't feel the same way? He thinks I'm moving too fast!* He curled his hands by his chest, scraping his chin along the back of one hand as he stared intently at his feet and wondered if he could disappear *into* the earth. "Was that too fast?"

"Wh-What? No," Henry said, sounding so surprised that Jaden blinked and stared up at him. He looked earnestly confused. "No, I just need to tell you something right now, before we go any further. A lot of shit went down."

Jaden's relief quickly vanished, replaced by an even more sickening feeling. Henry's voice had just wobbled on that last word. For once, it was Henry shrinking back—in voice, in personality, even physically—like he was afraid.

Afraid of what? What Jaden would think?

"What's wrong?" Jaden breathed out.

"My boss overheard me coming out to Trip. He scratched me from the schedule, and I confronted him." Henry's voice was strained, like it hurt to talk. "He said some transphobic shit, and basically I'm out of a job."

Jaden's jaw dropped. "What the *fuck?*"

"I know," Henry moaned, and he closed his eyes. "So I'm going to start my own outfit with Trip. But I want to be out from the start this time."

Jaden nodded wordlessly, still trying to process anything

other than his overwhelming urge to drop Damien into a trash can.

"But I don't know what this means," Henry breathed out. "I've come out to like, three people I know well. You, Trip, and Damien. I've got a point-three average for strike-outs, and I—I just—I don't know if you *want* that in your life."

Now, that was a bombshell. "*What?*" Jaden gasped. Henry sounded like he was trying to push him away now.

Could they get a do-over on today?

Henry was still talking, ticking off points on his fingers. "—and I don't want to go back into stealth mode, and I don't want to bring more trouble to you when that's already the thing that you're most afraid of—"

"No, you can't—he can't—no," Jaden snapped, sitting bolt upright.

Henry blinked at him. For some reason, he looked... even more confused now. "What?"

"What?" Jaden echoed. He sat up straight, every inch an indignant squirrel towering under the huge, lanky puppy beside him. "Look, I want to be with you. For the long haul. I basically just told you that. And I know you're hurting right now, but if this is *going* to work for the long haul, you gotta trust me to know my own mind, rather than put me in a bubble and assume things will hurt me. My mind, and my heart, and my soul, and my body, and every little bit of me agrees that *you're the one.* So I don't give a shit how many people have a problem with you, because I love you, and if I have to learn karate or some shit to deal with dickheads like your ex-boss, so help me God, I'll do it."

Then Jaden stopped, his own jaw dropping as he realized he'd just made... a speech. And confessed his love. And maybe threatened to knock out Henry's boss.

Silence rang between them for a few seconds.

At least Henry didn't respond with another, "What?" He just stared, his mouth hanging open wide enough to catch flies.

Jaden's cheeks flushed as he watched Henry's expression shift from frantic panic—a feeling he knew all too well—to disbelief, and finally something else completely.

Something that almost terrified Jaden to name, but made his heart sing in the crystal-clear tones he could no longer ignore.

Love.

Henry sagged against Jaden, a long breath rushing out of his lungs as he threw his arms around Jaden and squeezed him tightly. "I love you too, sweetheart."

Jaden squeaked quietly, burying his face in Henry's neck again. "I kinda hoped so. But I didn't plan to say any of that, either. I didn't want to seem too eager or anything, and…"

It was Henry's turn to chuckle gently. He pulled back and pressed a kiss against Jaden's lips, cutting off the worries that had threatened to build up like a thunderhead.

Suddenly nothing else mattered, except the way Henry kissed him deep and slow, and the intoxicating sweetness of his lips, and the way Jaden's heart thrilled every time Henry gently brushed his hand back through Jaden's hair.

"I *love* you," Henry repeated, his voice raw and eyes damp when he pulled back. "And that's been the point all along, isn't it? That we don't listen to anyone else's normal. I'm sorry for holding back all my worries. For trying to put you in a bubble. And for not seeing that you really needed me."

Jaden just nodded, drawing his knees up and resting them across Henry's lap. "And I'm sorry for not really telling you what was going on . For hiding it away instead of saying it was important."

"Me, too," Henry murmured. He kissed Jaden's temple softly. "But for the record, since I haven't said it yet: yes."

"Yes...?" Jaden blinked.

"Yes, I want you to move in with me. My house is big enough for all of us. I think you'll love it there." Henry's voice grew excited. "I'll show you today, if you want. And you can move in right now. Or whenever. I want to spend every day with you, my love."

Oh. Jaden was exhausted now in the aftermath of all his emotion. He just nuzzled into Henry's shoulder and whispered, "Thank you. I feel like I suck at relationships. Crying on a park bench was not how I pictured confessing my love."

A chuckle burst out of Henry as he rocked Jaden gently. "I'm not a pro at them, either. But we'll get better at it, hm? Together. No more second-guessing what the other one wants."

Jaden nodded and pressed his lips against Henry's. He didn't give a shit who saw them. Not today, anyway.

He just lost himself in the sweet softness of Henry's lips. Time passed like this—how much time exactly didn't matter.

Eventually, Cece loudly huffed a sigh from where she was lying next to the bench, making them break apart with laughter.

"So, wanna see your sweet new house?" Henry grinned.

"Yeah," Jaden whispered, brushing his hand along Henry's cheek and gazing into those bright blue pools of warmth and love.

He couldn't wait.

Twenty~Two

HENRY

IT WAS BARELY TWO WEEKS LATER, AND NEARLY EVERY DAY HAD been chaos. Either Henry was over at Jaden's place helping him pack, or he was out with Trip drawing up business plans and talking to people at the bank like a couple of pros who knew what they were doing.

Apparently they managed to fool enough people into thinking they were adults to get a business bank account, state guiding licenses, and a meeting with the local tourism department.

Even that would have been surreal enough. But now… watching Jaden walk into his beautiful home and casually toss his jacket on the hook in the front hallway?

Henry could hardly believe his luck.

Jaden had been practically living here for the past couple of weeks anyway. They'd both agreed he should move in right away rather than waiting for his lease to come up. Ron clearly wanted him out, and Jaden needed to leave.

Plus, what better time to learn to live together? They'd

fallen into an easy rhythm after the first week. Henry was just about used to having someone home when he got in from a long day of meetings. He could definitely get used to having a friendly face to greet him when he arrived back from a trip, exhausted and muddy.

Jaden set down the box he carried and turned to look at Henry. Then he grinned. "You're smiling at me like that again."

"Like what?" Henry's cheeks flushed as Jaden danced up to him on tiptoe and pressed a kiss on his lips.

"Like my heart feels right now," Jaden murmured.

"Oh, boy. Again?" They both turned and laughed as Spence came in, carrying two boxes and craning his neck to see around them.

Trip joined in, yelling from outside, "Tell them to get their asses out here and stop necking."

"Sorry," Henry said with a grin. He pecked Jaden on the lips again and waited for Spence to turn and head back out before smacking Jade's cute little ass.

Jaden gasped silently and pretended to be offended, but when Henry led the way, he got him back with a perfectly-placed pinch.

"Your turn dealing with the lovebirds," Trip said with a long-suffering sigh. "I've had to see this all week."

"Well, you *were* the ones who got us together," Jaden pointed out with a wicked grin. "So technically it's your own fault."

Spence pretended to sigh and roll his eyes, but Trip grinned. "I'm willing to accept the blame for that."

Henry lingered behind with Spence for a moment while the other two headed back with more boxes. "Thanks for helping us out today, man," he said. "I really appreciate it."

"Oh, no sweat." Spence wiped his forehead and laughed. "I mean, lots of sweat, but you've got the beer, right?"

Henry chuckled. "Of course. And pizza." He'd save the wild salads with foraged ingredients for Jaden. Henry had the feeling he'd appreciate them more than Trip and Spence after moving day. Carbs were where it was at.

At least Jaden and his brother were getting along a lot better now that Spence didn't have to shop for groceries and help him with everything so much.

Cece had been a godsend, too. Jaden had gone to the corner store a few times with her since moving in, and now that the staff all knew her, they didn't give them any trouble.

"It's nice to see you guys happy," Spence said with a nod, grabbing another box from the back of the truck. "My girlfriend and I just split up a couple days ago, so…"

Henry stopped. "Oh! Sorry, man."

"No, no." Spence smiled in the direction of the house. "I'm glad it happened. I didn't like who I was becoming. Kicking Jaden out of the nest, getting selfish all of a sudden when he was really counting on me. She was really pushing me away from him, and nobody should do that. I'm a dick for not seeing it sooner."

Henry didn't quite know what to say. Yeah, part of him had wanted to chew Spence out over those first few days, but it seemed like he and Jaden were in a much better place now. "We all learn. Sometimes the hard way."

Spence nodded, then reached out and squeezed Henry's shoulder. "I'll try to be less of a jerk when I get back to dating. And in the meantime… I'm really happy he has you around to count on. Our parents are going to love you."

Henry's face must have been horrified, because Spence

just laughed again. "I was trying not to get ahead of myself," Henry admitted.

"Nah, don't worry about it. I promise they will. Anyone who makes my baby bro happy." Spence smiled at him for a moment before shoving a box into his arms. "Now let's get this thing unpacked so we can crack open the beer."

"Hear, hear."

It didn't take long before the living room was filled with an assortment of boxes. The open, airy layout looked terrifyingly cluttered all of a sudden, but Henry had a feeling those boxes weren't going to stay packed for long.

Already, Jaden was rummaging around for something. When he pulled it out and turned it around to show the others, Spence tilted his head and Trip leaned in, setting aside his beer bottle.

"Oh, my God."

Henry had completely forgotten the awkward photo they'd taken with the little H2H sign—for promotional purposes—right after landing in Phoenix.

Somehow, Jaden had gotten his hands on a copy of the photo—and his raffle ticket stub, which was tucked into the frame.

They looked so dorky, arms around each other's shoulders, fixed smiles on their faces, clutching the sign between them.

Jaden blushed, fidgeting with the frame. "I thought this could go on the mantle...?"

"Yeah. That's perfect," Henry murmured. He blushed from head to toe and set down his beer bottle, rummaging in his pocket for his wallet. "I... still have mine, too," he admitted.

Sure enough, there it was—tucked in the very corner where he wouldn't lose it.

Jaden added it to the corner of the frame and set it down, then hopped back over the boxes to sit next to Henry again. "Perfect," he whispered.

"Well, jeez." Trip swiped at his eyes. "Now you're not allowed to give me any more feelings until the wedding, all right?"

Jaden squeaked while Henry choked on his beer, and the laughter that went around the room swept the moment away. But Henry caught Jaden side-eyeing him with a coy little smile, and he met it with a grin of his own.

Yeah. That sounded pretty damn good to him, too.

"My little brother might beat me to the married life," Spence said, pretending to pout.

"Aww. I'll be your consolation prize," Trip told him, leaning into him while Spence elbowed him and complained, but they were both laughing.

"Maybe I should say yes." Spence chuckled. "Not sure I trust my taste in women anymore."

"You never know," Trip said. "You could fall head over heels for someone. It happens, I've been told." He winked at Jaden and Henry.

Spence looked thoughtful for a moment. "How about Buckle next weekend, the four of us? Double date? This deserves a party." Before anyone else answered, he held up a finger and looked at his little brother. "Jaden, what do you say?"

Jaden gave him a grin of relief and a little nod. "You know what? I think I can do it. Just for a couple of hours."

Trip whooped and held up his beer. "I'm in."

Henry grinned and put his arm around Jaden. "I can't wait."

If Jaden got overwhelmed, they could come back home

and dance all on their own, with nobody else watching. Nobody to spill drinks on them or shout over. Just them, slow-dancing the night away, every night they could.

Whatever lay ahead in life, he couldn't wait to find out.

Twenty~Three

JADEN

Jaden was worn out, bruised, and happier than he could remember. Cece was fast asleep downstairs in her new bed, and he couldn't quite believe he was living somewhere that *had* a downstairs.

He was so lucky to get this opportunity to build something new and precious with Henry.

And speaking of precious, Henry was spoiling him with a bubble bath for two. The tub was big, but not *that* big, so he squeezed between Henry's knees and rested his back against Henry's chest.

Right now, his boyfriend was rubbing all the knots and aches from his neck, his wet hands trailing gently across Jaden's skin.

Jaden was warm, contented, and utterly pleased as he swished his hands around his knees in the water. "We can do this more often," he suggested with a smile. It was such a treat to have a bathtub after living for years with only a shower.

Even more of a treat to share it with the handsome man he now shared his home and life with.

"I'll keep the request on file," Henry teased and kissed Jaden's shoulder. Then he mouthed at Jaden's neck before closing his lips around the rim of Jaden's ear.

Jaden gasped, squirming and rubbing his back against Henry's shaft. "Are you trying to wake me up?"

"Can't let you fall asleep," Henry growled playfully, sliding both hands down Jaden's chest and pulling him in even closer. "That's dangerous."

Pressed so tightly against Henry's shaft, Jaden was definitely not sleepy now. He licked his lips and moaned. If he was going to make a habit of asking for what he needed, why not start now? "Would you make love to me tonight? I think I can handle Henry Huge."

Henry laughed, nuzzling Jaden's neck. "Is that your nickname for him?"

"Yup. Every great dick needs a nickname." Maybe the heat and exhaustion were making Jaden loopy, but oh, how his heart soared at Henry's laugh.

"I'd be delighted to take you to bed, my love." Henry's fingers walked up Jaden's abs and over his chest. He caressed both nipples at once, rolling them between his thumbs and index fingers.

Like an instrument springing to life in the hands of a musician, Jaden throbbed with desire. He cried out softly, gripping the edges of the tub as he tried to steady his breathing.

But it was no good. He was putty in Henry's hands, trembling against him and crying out with each new touch Henry tried.

His cock wasn't floating aimlessly anymore, that was for sure.

"Looks like someone's waking up," Henry said, low and playful. He grazed his palms over Jaden's stomach and into the water, gently cupping Jaden's cock in his hands. He playfully pushed it down and let it spring up again, sluicing through the water with a pleasurable jolt.

"Two can play at that game," Jaden murmured. He tried to grope behind him at Henry, but the tub was too small, and all he wound up doing was giggling and splashing bubbles everywhere as he squirmed in Henry's hold.

"Come on. Let's not cause a flood," Henry suggested, grinning impishly. He carefully took Jaden by the waist, helping him stand up. But he didn't let Jaden leave the tub yet, just wolf-whistling at the view. "Bend over."

Jaden choked on his gasp and obeyed, bracing his hands on the taps.

The cooling air on his wet skin was quickly forgotten as Henry's warm tongue traced a line from Jaden's balls, across his taint, and right to the sensitive little hole he so desperately wanted filled tonight.

"Fuck," Jaden hissed, the water sloshing around his feet as he braced himself.

Henry moaned against him, gently sucking the rim around his puckered entrance, then lapping across it in short, quick strokes. Aching with need and rock-hard, Jaden cried out, his knees trembling.

He craved Henry sliding deep inside, stretching him open and claiming him.

"Fuck me," Jaden begged in a mumble, his face in the crook of his elbow as he clung to the taps for dear life.

"Hmm?" Henry hummed against the opening and then gently pushed the tip of his tongue inside.

Jaden's cry was raw and guttural. "Fuck me," he whimpered, his voice stronger. "I need you inside me now, Henry."

Henry finally pulled away, kissing his thighs and sliding his hands up to Jaden's waist again. "Out you get."

Jaden grabbed the edge of the tub until he was sure his legs were strong enough, then stepped out. Henry followed, pulling the plug and grabbing towels from a shelf nearby. He didn't just hand Jaden a towel—he unfolded it himself and rubbed it along Jaden's sides and back, enveloping him in the fluffy fabric.

Jaden breathed out a trembling, yearning sigh as Henry wrapped the towel around him. The soft fabric grazed the hard, sensitive tip of his shaft. He draped the towel around his shoulders and then reached out to help Henry dry off, too.

"You're so damn hot," Jaden breathed out, using the ends of the towel to rub Henry's chest. He pressed firmly, not afraid of overstimulating him now that he knew where the nerve endings were dull.

Henry grinned at him, reaching between his legs to squeeze himself. As his shaft grew thicker and harder, Jaden bit back his whimper of need. His own towel was good and tented, the exhaustion that had sat in his bones earlier thoroughly gone.

They couldn't keep their hands off each other, helping each other towel dry. Henry's palms gliding over his body, even with the towel blocking some of these sensations, made Jaden quiver pleasantly.

When they were dry enough, they tugged away each

other's towels with laughter and then made for the bedroom, closing the door firmly in case Cece got ideas.

Jaden hit the bed face-first and scrambled up to the pillows before turning onto his back and raising his knees to his chest.

Henry bit his lip as he looked him up and down, then grabbed lube and crawled over Jaden like a predator who had seen his very favorite meal. He pressed a long, hot kiss against Jaden's lips before slicking his fingers.

"Yes," Jaden whispered, his body quivering in anticipation. "Lots of fingering, please."

Henry chuckled gently and kissed his knee, hoisting Jaden's legs over his shoulders. "Of course, baby. I don't want to hurt you."

"I've never had anything as big in me before," Jaden admitted breathlessly. "But I can't wait."

He was *almost* sure he could handle that thick shaft inside him. And he was completely sure he needed it.

"Me too," Henry whispered. His touch was loving and delicate as he pushed a slick finger into Jaden, kissing him softly to help him ease into it.

Jaden lost himself in Henry's kisses, sucking at his lips and crying out gently against his mouth as Henry added a finger. It was slow and tender, yet the sharp edge of excitement never left. It felt like he'd been waiting forever for this moment.

And it was finally here. Henry sat back on his heels and squeezed more wetness into his palm, then stroked himself slowly. He gave Jaden a wolfish grin when he noticed him watching and slowed down, making it a show.

"Don't make me come just watching you," Jaden warned with a breathless laugh. "That's a real danger."

Henry grinned. "That would be a shame," he agreed, taking his erect shaft in hand and rubbing the head around the slick, waiting hole.

"Now," Jaden gasped, begging or perhaps commanding—whatever would win Henry over.

The sharp sting and heat of Henry pushing into him made Jaden cry out, clutching at the cool blankets by his sides. It hurt, but God, did it ever burn in the best possible way.

"You okay?" Henry whispered, his touch running across Jaden's thigh.

"P-Perfect," Jaden managed, his eyes squeezed closed.

Slowly and tenderly, Henry eased into Jaden until his gasps grew too sharp and then stopped, rubbing his body all over and waiting patiently for him to be ready again.

Henry filled Jaden's needy, aching hole completely, stretching him beyond his limits and into another place he'd never been. He'd never been a size queen before, but goddamn, Jaden suddenly understood why girth was important.

"It's so damn good," Jaden whimpered, covering his face. "Oh my God." His cock was flushing with heat and stiffness again, his body starting to prickle impatiently.

He needed Henry to move.

Henry chuckled, folding him in two as he leaned down for another kiss and pulled Jaden's knees closer to his ears. "You're doing so well," he praised softly. "You feel so fucking incredible."

"What's it like?" Jaden whispered, his eyes flickering open so he could admire Henry. The man's cheeks were flushed, his eyes positively sparkling.

"Perfect." Henry's gaze was soft and reverent. "I'm making

love to a man—my very own boyfriend—with nothing in the way. Nothing else but our bodies." His voice trembled with emotion, his hands sliding carefully up to Jaden's shoulders as he leaned down to kiss him again. "Perfect," he repeated.

Jaden whimpered, clenching around the length that practically split him open. "You're so big," he gasped. "Stop me if I'm repeating myself, but God. It's incredible. I feel like I'm splitting in two, but in the best way."

The hot bursts of sparks that shot through him sure helped. Each time the head of Henry's cock slid across his prostate, Jaden's whole body trembled and went taut like a drum.

He could hardly breathe, the sparks had built into such an unquenchable thirst. "Harder," Jaden begged, clutching at Henry's back and digging in his nails. "Please."

And Henry obeyed, thrusting into him in short movements at first, then deepening it. "You're so hot when you squeeze around my cock. When you take it all." He pressed breathless kisses against Jaden's lips. "Tell me what you feel, too."

"My love," Jaden whispered, his chest positively bursting with the glow that felt like it radiated through his whole body. Like he'd turned into the sun itself.

"No," Henry teased with a peck on his cheek. "That's your prostate."

Jaden giggled and didn't stop until Henry shifted his angle and pounded into him, harder and faster than before. Then his laughter turned to soft cries—and then louder.

Being silly during sex was something he'd never thought was allowed, but now? It just felt natural.

"Yes!" Jaden cried out, his moans thick and fast. "Yes, baby, fuck me. Hard. Please. I need you!"

Henry growled and bit Jaden's lower lip, grabbing his hands and pinning them over his head. His other forearm braced by Jaden's head, he slammed into him hard and fast.

The unbearable pressure inside couldn't last much longer. Jaden whimpered and cried with every thrust, the plateau of joy suddenly cresting until it threatened to block out every other thought.

Nothing else in the world mattered but Henry inside him, filling him up, *taking* him.

"I'm—*Henry*," Jaden gasped, urgent and ragged. His eyes flew open, his body telling the whole story. He clenched and quivered around Henry's hot, firm shaft, squirming under him as he finally let go.

Bliss struck, and Jaden cried out as his muscles squeezed hard before letting go in sudden, intense jolts. He bucked off the bed, pushing up into Henry as his legs slid off his shoulders.

His own hot mess splattered across his chest, droplets of passion landing on his collarbone and painting his nipples.

"Fuck," Henry gasped, easing out of him. He knelt there, letting go of Jaden's wrists and grabbing hold of himself, stroking hard and fast. "Feeling you come is just..." He suddenly gasped, his eyes closing before he threw his head back. "Yes!"

Henry's hips bucked forward, the head of his cock sliding between the ridges of his fingers in stuttering thrusts as his whole body shuddered and he gasped for air.

Jaden was spellbound, his hands resting on Henry's shoulders as he drank in every moment.

He could watch Henry coming over and over again. He wanted to memorize all the ripples of his muscles and his gorgeous body, his face pinching tight and pretty, thin lips gasping for breath.

Finally, Henry stopped stroking and grabbed the bed, still breathing hard. His eyes fluttered open, hazy and stunned.

Jaden beamed up at him, guiding him down to cuddle. His ass ached, but goddamn, it felt incredible. "Good, I presume?"

"I gotta try that again and see if it's like this every time," Henry murmured. "If so, I hope you're up for it every day."

"Please," Jaden breathed, squirming under Henry's hot, rock-hard body. "Tomorrow morning? It's the perfect excuse to keep me limber. Wouldn't want to get moving-day pains."

Henry giggled softly and kissed him. "Oh, I love you, Jaden."

"I love you too," Jaden whispered, beaming at him. "And if you feel wandering hands in the middle of the night... I'm just making sure we've both got morning wood."

"Oh, trust me," Henry murmured with a devilish wink. "We will."

They kissed gently now as they cuddled, coming down from the high until they could both breathe again.

"With you," Henry murmured at last, catching Jaden's attention, "I feel like I'll figure out everything I need to. Maybe not everything will go right, but that's okay."

"Yeah?" Jaden whispered, peeking up at Henry as he nuzzled his chest.

Henry smiled down at him, soft and amazed. "I'm free."

Jaden couldn't believe he put it so perfectly. He was going to keep building up evidence for his brain that things would be okay. And sure, there would be setbacks... but things would never again be the same.

Everything was different, and *he* was different, too. He'd

grown a lot in the past years, and more so in these past few months than ever.

With Henry's belief in him, Jaden could believe in himself a little bit more. He finally trusted himself to have the tools he needed to make his life work.

Maybe that was what he'd missed all along: he'd been so focused on trying to avoid bad things that he'd stopped trusting himself to deal with them.

"Me, too," Jaden whispered at last, shaking his head with contentment. "Thank you for believing in me."

Henry chuckled softly and kissed his cheek, his strong arms wrapping around Jaden. Like nothing in the world could ever come between them again.

In each other, they'd finally found freedom.

Epilogue

JADEN

"You doing okay?"

It was a now-familiar refrain, and every time Henry said it, Jaden still smiled. Henry was always by his side when he needed him.

That included when they were out hiking in the mountains—which were considerably less scorching than their very first hike had been. Denver's mountains were just as wide-open and terrifying as the Nevada scrubland, though.

Their third time trying this hike seemed to be the charm. At last, with Henry by his side, Jaden had been able to enjoy the scenery.

Spence was over the moon, too. When he visited, they were brothers again—bantering and joking around. Together with Trip, they'd all gone to Buckle last week and had a truly great night.

Today, Jaden and Henry were hiking in the early morning, just after sunrise. There had only been two other cars in the parking area, and they hadn't run into either hiking group.

With Henry's hand in his, Jaden could focus on his breathing and remind himself that he was just as safe here as he was at home.

He was a long way from feeling like he once had, but in the months since meeting Henry, he'd made tremendous progress.

Moving from his little apartment to Henry's spacious house had been the change Jaden needed. Not just so he didn't have to leave the house to see Henry—but so he felt more confident leaving the house in general.

It let him listen in on more of Henry's business planning. He and Trip were pulling together plans for Along the Rainbow's first trans summer camp—which was finally happening next week.

Hell, Jaden was confident enough about this hike that he'd let Cereal off-lead, which meant she was off-duty to enjoy the open space. She'd been making rapid strides in her training, and was close to ready to fully be a service dog.

She caught up with them and bounded ahead, barking vigorously at stones on the path, her fur stuck out at wild angles.

"You're ridiculous," Jaden laughed at Cece.

"Oh, no—" Henry started, but they couldn't call her back in time.

She'd found a muddy stream bed, and she was immediately on her back, all four paws in the air, a dopey grin on her face as she squirmed in it.

So much for her golden fur. That tub was going to need serious rinsing after her bath. Jaden found himself laughing so much at her antics that he almost forgot to be nervous.

Every damn morning waking up with this man, he felt blessed. Jaden loved trying to pump Henry Huge to full mast, while Henry retaliated by turning him on in inappropriate public places.

Their antics always ended up in squirming giggles, wrestling, and smoking hot sex.

"I know that smirk." Henry eyed Jaden, but he was grinning. "It's too cold out here."

"Are you sure?"

"Being *able* to keep it up doesn't mean being turned on!" Henry laughed.

Jaden smirked. "Yeah, but…" He reached for Henry, who was expecting him to make a playful grab for his nuts. Instead, he squeezed his ass and then sprinted ahead.

"Oh!" Henry gasped and then gave chase, his laughter betraying exactly how far he was behind him. "It's so on!"

Cereal bounding around their ankles and doing her best to trip them both up, Jaden sprinted into the mountains with his boyfriend at his back, his dog by his side, and a taste of hard-won freedom on his tongue.

Wait—where had the trail gone? They were at a clearing, and he couldn't see a path ahead. He did see a slab of rock with a metal disk embedded, though.

Henry caught up with him, out of breath and laughing. "We're here!"

"We're… here?" He'd made it to the top? Jaden caught his breath, his smile growing. It wasn't a huge mountain or arduous trek, but it was so much further than he'd gone in years.

Jaden's face almost split with a smile. His cheeks hurt as he grabbed Henry and hugged him, and Henry wrapped those strong arms around him.

Home was where Henry was.

There was a bench up here, so Henry pulled Jaden to sit

down and then shrugged off his backpack to set out the breakfast they'd cooked together.

As they each grabbed a bacon and egg English muffin, Henry put his hand on Jaden's knee. His smile asked the question again with no need for words.

The hope in Jaden's heart shone that much brighter in response. He beamed at Henry and the world that stretched beyond him. "Couldn't be better."

Afterword

Thank you for reading Freedom! The F-Word books are among those closest to my heart, and it means a lot to share the stories I need to see.

It was deeply important to me to write a story about a trans man post-bottom surgery, as there are still so many myths and fears out there but so few informative personal experiences about the everyday reality of phalloplasty.

If reading my work raised any questions on this or other subjects, please be aware that a great deal of negative information is deliberately propagated and be cautious about the sources of information you seek out. GLAAD is a good resource to begin learning more: glaad.org/transgender/transFAQ

Much of my inspiration came from my own life—and what a journey it's been! I owe a great deal of thanks to my found family, who have surrounded and supported me with so much love throughout this wild ride.

I want to acknowledge in particular my tremendous debt to my elders—all those who have come before me and who fought for our rights. In particular, the little-known trail-blazer Lou Sullivan advocated for medical reform on behalf of gay trans men. Without him, I wouldn't have been allowed to live my own authentic life, much less come so far as to write this book.

There are an infinite number of possible trans identities and lives. This story is just one tiny sliver of the beautiful tapestry that is trans people. I encourage you to seek out other books to learn about them.

MM romance featuring trans men is growing more common; my previous books include *Grind*, *Flaunt*, and *Forever*.

There are also many brilliant nonfiction books about trans lives; my recommendations include *Trans Like Me* by CN Lester, *decolonizing trans/gender 101* by b. binaohan, and *Gender Explorers* by Juno Roche.

If you haven't already, make sure you sign up to my newsletter: edaviesbooks.com/subscribe You'll hear about freebies and deals; new releases in ebook, audio, and print; preorder alerts; sneak peeks at upcoming books; event appearances; and other exciting news as it happens!

I also have a reader group on Facebook if you want to chat about your favorite parts of *Freedom*, see cute bee photos and good news stories, and keep on top of my upcoming releases with a whole bunch of lovely readers: facebook.com/groups/edavies

Always be you!

~Ed

About the Author

E. Davies writes feel-good, low-angst romance that never fades to black when the going gets good! Born in Canada, after 16 moves and counting, Ed has finally put down roots in north London.

He emerges from his writing nest to coo over fuzzy animals, flee from cute guys, dance through the streets with his chosen family, put together fierce looks, and—most of all—befriend local flowers.

You can find all available titles at: www.edaviesbooks.com

Follow E. Davies online:

amazon.com/author/edavies
bookbub.com/authors/e-davies
facebook.com/edaviesauthor
goodreads.com/edavies
instagram.com/edaviesauthor
x.com/edaviesauthor

Also by E. Davies

Sunrise Island Brothers:

Collide

Stranded

Hart's Bay:

Hard Hart

Changed Hart

Wild Hart

Stolen Hart

Significant Brothers:

Splinter

Grasp

Slick

Trace

Clutch

Tremble

Riley Brothers:

Buzz

Clang

Swish

Crunch

Slam

Grind

Brooklyn Boys:

Electric Sunshine

Live Wire

Boiling Point

F-Word:

Flaunt

Freak

Faux

Forever

Freedom

After:

Afterburn

Afterglow

Aftermath

Shared Universes:

Shelter

Adore

Miracle

Redemption

Limelight

Barely Regal